Boom, Bang, and A Body

A Sydney Hayes Mystery

Book 3

Misty Lynn

ACKNOWLEDGMENTS

I want to thank my family and friends for their love and support throughout my writing journey. Who would have thought I'd make it this far? Woo-hoo—book three is complete! I am especially grateful to my reading group and new beta readers, Penny and Amy, for helping me catch grammatical errors and polish my book. I also want to thank Dan for sharing his expertise and helping me understand the intricacies of tattooing. Lastly, I extend my sincere appreciation to the brave men and women of the armed forces. Thank you for your dedication and service to our country.

Books in the Sydney Hayes series

Hometown Murder
Mischief in the Morgue
Boom, Bang, and a Body

CHAPTER 1

It was a hot, airless summer day in Pennsylvania. The kind so sweltering that even the trees were looking for shade. Usually, on a day like this, I would find refuge indoors, savoring the cool embrace of air conditioning. But with the desire to soak in local events during my visit, I decided to step outside.

So here I was, downtown, for the dedication of the newly repaired bell in the church belfry. As I strolled toward the church, I felt an unexpected thrill of anticipation. The bell, which had been silent for over forty years, was ready to ring again. Today marked a momentous occasion for the town, and the first time most of us would hear its angelic tone.

Upon arriving downtown, I was surprised by the overwhelming size of the crowd. It appeared as though the entire town had turned out, huddled under the bright sun in front of the church. The main street had been roped off to traffic for the event.

Several food trucks lined the street, their enticing aromas wafting through the humid air. Yet it was the small lemonade stand in front of the police station that caught my attention. A long line snaked its way towards the rickety stand, which was haphazardly constructed from two aging sawhorses topped with a weathered plank of wood. It looked like it would fall apart if someone merely leaned on it.

The lemonade must be exceptional to draw such a crowd, so I took my place in line.

"You know the church steeple is the tallest building in town," came a voice from behind me.

I turned around to find Dixie standing there. She was an elderly lady with more wrinkles than Leatherface and silver spikey hair with purple tips. She was a friend of my grandmother's, and we recently watched over her dog while she was away.

"They did that on purpose," she continued. "So that the sound of the bell would travel all the way through town. Back then, few people owned clocks, so the bell served as their timekeeper."

"Interesting," I replied, fanning myself with my hand as the summer sun bore down. I tugged at the hem of my tank top, trying to catch a breath of cool air while beads of sweat trickled beneath my spandex sports bra.

Suddenly, someone switched on the microphone, and the piercing screech filled the air, making me wince. Thankfully, after a few excruciating seconds, Father Michael stepped up to the podium and silenced it.

"I went to school with Father Michael," Dixie said, her voice holding a hint of nostalgia.

"Back when Lincoln was president?" I teased.

She slapped me on the arm. "Don't be cheeky."

The line at the lemonade stand moved quickly. It was run by two girls in their teens and one young girl. All three girls had the same curly chestnut hair, hinting at the fact that they were sisters. I stepped in front of the taller teenager, her expression looking bored.

"One please," I said.

"Leaded or unleaded?" she responded, a sly smile tugging at her lips as she discreetly clutched a vodka bottle hidden beneath the edge of the stand.

I raised an eyebrow. "Aren't you a little young to be selling alcohol on a public sidewalk? Especially right in front of the police station?"

"Whatever," she replied with a casual shrug. "How do you want it?"

I only debated it for a second. "Leaded."

Maybe some alcohol would make being around this many people more bearable. I had always preferred the shadows, content to melt into the background, possibly explaining why I excelled in my work.

She handed me a plastic cup, the kind that crinkled when you grasped it, and I made my way across the street to get a better view of the ceremony. At the top of the church stairs, a solitary microphone stood next to the podium which was flanked by two imposing speakers.

I lifted the cup to my lips and took a sip, only to erupt in a cough. It contained more vodka than lemonade. If you could even call it lemonade, as it tasted more like watered down alcohol. The alcohol taste was so strong, I was starting to wonder if it was alcohol in the bottle or homemade moonshine. I suspected the crowd was drawn to it since it was the only alcohol available on the street, even if it was illegally being served. At least it had some refreshingly cold ice in it.

"I see you decided to brave the local festivities," a familiar voice interrupted my thoughts.

I spun around to find Blake standing behind me.

"The festivities can't be that bad."

"I heard Gina was participating," he countered, raising an eyebrow as if to challenge my optimism. "Do you really think it won't turn into a problem with her involved?"

As I contemplated his words, he leaned closer and took a sniff of my drink. "I see you got the leaded version," he remarked.

I was shocked. "You know those kids are serving alcohol, and you're just turning a blind eye?" Right in front of the police station, no less. The irony hung in the air. Blake always seemed to stick with the law-black or white, no exception.

He shrugged. "Their father's an alcoholic with a bad temper that could ignite a wildfire. Cleaning out the liquor stash from their home would bring some much-needed peace to this town, at least for a little while."

The microphone screeched on again, and Father Michael blew into it to check the sound. It was so loud that it sounded like I was standing in a wind tunnel during a raging hurricane. He quickly shut it back off.

"At least I can relax today knowing you're staying out of trouble," Blake said.

I planted my hands on my hips defiantly. "I haven't caused any trouble since setting foot in this town."

"You may not have started any trouble, but you certainly have a knack for finding yourself right in the thick of it," he said, leaning toward me with a teasing glint in his eyes. "And it appears that a few pink specks have taken up residence in your hair."

Several weeks ago, I opened a package that turned out to be a glitter bomb. The tiny, sticky particles clung stubbornly to my skin, refusing to be washed off for days. I wouldn't be at all surprised if remnants of Blake's prank weren't still woven into my hair, shimmering under the light.

Before I could respond with a snide comment, a voice rang out calling my name. I turned and saw a man striding toward me across the street. He radiated an air of confidence and arrogance with each step. Even after not seeing him for a decade, he appeared unchanged. It was Chase Mathis.

Chase was the high school quarterback that every girl wanted to date. My sister swore he was every bit as handsome as Brad Pitt, with his chiseled jawline and piercing blue eyes. He was never short of admirers, and he never cast a second glance in my direction. I couldn't help but wonder why he was seeking me out now.

"Try to stay out of trouble, Army," Blake called over his shoulder as he disappeared into the crowd.

"Sydney, you look stunning," Chase said, reaching for my hand and gently squeezing it.

"Chase, nice to see you," I said, quickly extracting my hand from his grasp. With my dirty blonde hair pulled back into a simple ponytail and my outfit consisting of a tank top and side-pocketed cargo shorts, I wasn't convinced of his sincerity. I wanted to hurl at his failed attempt to pique my interest.

"I heard you were back in town," he continued eagerly. "I was hoping to run into you." He ran his fingers through his sandy blond hair, then gave it a casual shake as if each hair had to fall into its perfect place.

It was an effort not to roll my eyes at his antics.

Music started playing from the speaker in front of the church, signaling the beginning of the ceremony.

"We must get together soon. I'll be in touch," he said. He winked at me and walked away before I could utter a protest. I shook my head, redirecting my focus to the church.

The building loomed before me, constructed from sturdy grey stone that whispered of history and endurance. Its towering steeple shot upwards and from within its grand opening hung a magnificent gold bell that glinted in the light. The steeple was crowned by a vibrant emerald green metal roof, with a polished silver cross perched on top. I remembered that the roof was once white, but I was told it was replaced several years ago. They chose green when they replaced it to give the building a splash of color.

As the massive wooden doors opened, three women emerged. Their attire transporting them back to the elegance of the nineteenth century. They were followed by the two nuns who dwelt at the church. Gina was among them dressed in a beautiful peach-colored evening gown with a neckline that dropped off her shoulders. The neckline, adorned with delicate ivory pleats, highlighted her graceful neck, while the sleeves were short and flirtatious. She held a matching peach parasol over her shoulder which added a whimsical touch to her appearance. The wide hoop skirts of all three women fanned out around them, making them stand a distance apart.

All three women waved gracefully to the crowd. As Gina slipped back inside the church, the sunlight glinted off the stained-glass windows, casting colorful patterns on the ground. Meanwhile, the other two women positioned themselves behind Father Michael.

"Thank you all for coming to show your support," Father Michael began, his voice resonating. "As you know, we are gathered here to dedicate the newly restored church bell. Thanks to our beloved late Pearl Razner's generous donation, we can again enjoy the sweet chime of this bell that has long been silent."

The ripple of applause washed over the crowd, along with a few enthusiastic cheers. Father Michael raised his hand, and the crowd fell silent once more. "The dedicated crew worked tirelessly to ensure the bell would be ready before the big annual Fourth of July Gettysburg reenactment."

I couldn't help but roll my eyes at the mention of the event. Every year, thousands of tourists flocked to my hometown for the yearly celebration of the Battle of Gettysburg, which took place during the Civil War over the first few days of July. When I was young, I purposely avoided town during this celebration, and this year would be no exception.

As the two nuns stepped away from the church, seeking a better view of the belfry, Sister Mary Sarah blew her whistle, a sharp sound that cut through the murmurs of the crowd. Within moments, Gina emerged from the belfry, her figure silhouetted against the bright sky. She waved to the onlookers, her smile radiating warmth and excitement.

I gulped, my heart racing with apprehension. After all the instances where Gina had landed herself in unexpected predicaments, the sight of her perched in the steeple ten stories above the ground was nothing short of nerve-wracking.

After Father Michael said a short dedication prayer he glanced at his watch. "It's time," he announced.

The crowd fell silent as they anticipated the first chime. When it finally came, it wasn't the melodic chime of a bell I expected but rather a deep, thunderous bang that reverberated through the very core of my being, making my teeth chatter. A few startled individuals in the crowd instinctively covered their ears, and I could hear at least one baby crying.

Up in the bell tower, Gina was caught off guard and covered her ears. She backed away from the bell as the resonant boom echoed around her. My breath caught in my throat as one of her feet slipped dangerously off the narrow ledge, the other teetering precariously on the edge. She flailed her arms in a desperate attempt to regain her balance but to no avail. I watched in horror as she lost her grip and tumbled from the tower.

CHAPTER 2

As she plummeted towards the ground, the crowd collectively gasped. A mix of terror and awe rippling through them. A few startled voices broke the tension with frantic screams. Thinking fast, Gina opened her parasol. With the parasol and the voluminous hoop skirt catching air, her descent slowed dramatically, and she glided gracefully like Mary Poppins. It appeared as if she would land softly in front of the church steps.

Suddenly, an unexpected gust of wind swept through, viciously redirecting her trajectory toward the two unsuspecting nuns. I dashed across the street towards the nuns. Sister Mary Sarah shrieked, her instincts kicking in as she managed to leap out of the way just in time. But Sister Evelyne Marie was not as fortunate.

As she turned to flee, she crashed straight into the lemonade stand. There was a loud cracking noise as the stand buckled beneath her weight, the one wooden sawhorse gave way and sent the plank clattering to the ground. Unfortunately, the other sawhorse stood its ground, so when Sister Evelyne collided with it, she toppled over it headfirst. Her skirt flew up over her head, revealing a pair of vibrant hot pink panties with the words 'Kiss this' written across the butt.

"Cool," one teenager at the booth exclaimed, a wide grin spreading across her face, while the other shrugged with a resigned "bummer" at the loss of their lemonade stand. In an instant, they both whipped out their cellphones, eager to catch the moment to share on social media. Father Michael was fervently performing the sign of the cross as he sprinted towards the disgraced nun.

Gina was ten feet from the ground when the wind lifted her back up like a hot air balloon and carried her across the street. I quickly adjusted my course, but it was too late; Gina descended swiftly, crashing down onto Lucinda with surprising force, sending them both sprawling onto the pavement. Lucinda was sprawled out on the concrete face down, while Gina sat atop her back like she had just beaten her in a prize fight.

Gina lifted her arms in the air and whooped.

"Get her off of me!" Lucinda screamed.

As I bent down to assist Gina, I cast a glance across the street, curious about Sister Evelyn Marie's predicament. Her face was flushed a deep crimson. She hastily tugged her skirt down to its proper place and scurried back toward the church.

I helped Gina to her feet and then reached down to retrieve her parasol. As I prepared to fold it, I noticed the unexpected metal brackets reinforcing the ribs inside—an intriguing detail that made me smile.

Meanwhile, Sean ambled over to Lucinda, extending his hand to help her stand. She brushed aside his offer with a dismissive flick and defiantly sprang to her feet. "You are a menace," she shouted at Gina. "You should be arrested!"

"For falling out of a bell tower?" Sean replied, raising an eyebrow skeptically.

"Absolutely," she insisted vehemently. "And for causing the desecration of Sister Evelyn. That poor nun may never step foot outside the parish again."

Sean shook his head. "I can't arrest someone for causing an accident, even if it's traumatic," he said.

"Yeah," I responded, a smirk tugging at the corners of my mouth. "Or your parents would have been arrested years ago for having you."

Gina giggled.

Lucinda flushed crimson and stomped her foot in frustration. "This isn't over," she squealed. "Rodney will hear about this." She turned on her heels and strode away with a huff.

"I don't know why she thinks that since her husband is the mayor she can run this town," Gina said.

"Here comes Krista," Sean said, waving to her.

I turned around and saw my sister coming our way. For a moment, she wore a radiant smile directed at Sean. But as soon as her gaze landed on me, her smile evaporated. She altered her course and hurried across the street.

Sean sighed. "I guess you won't shed any light on what's going on between the two of you?"

I shook my head. "Hopefully, it will work itself out soon."

"I hope so, too," Sean replied. "She hasn't been her cheerful self in weeks. I should get back to work."

As he walked away, my shoulders slumped. Glancing at Gina, I asked, "Do you think she'll ever forgive me?"

I had lied to my sister and my entire family about my job. They believed I was a flight nurse in the army when in reality, I worked in counterintelligence. That secret came crashing down several weeks ago when, by sheer accident, my sister uncovered the truth. She stormed out of the house and my life and hasn't spoken to me since. The worst part was the look of betrayal she flashed me before leaving. I should never have lied to her for so long.

"I know it may take some time, but I promise she will eventually forgive you."

"I hope it's sooner rather than later. I'll only be in town for another month or so."

I had returned to my hometown to recover from an injury I sustained during my last mission. A couple of bullets in the chest would slow anyone down. The military gave me the summer off to heal, and I could only hope that by the end of that time, I would regain my full strength and abilities before returning to the life I had chosen.

"By the way," I said to Gina as we strolled to the parking lot, "your fake fall from the bell tower was impressive. Did you enjoy yourself?"

Her eyes sparkled with excitement as she skipped alongside me, bouncing lightly on her feet. "It was epic. I always wanted to dramatically free-fall out of something high. Taking out Lucinda when I landed was the cherry on top."

I chuckled, shaking my head. "You're lucky you didn't end up breaking something, like your neck."

She waved me off with a dismissive hand. "I replaced the plastic bars with steel. There was no way that parasol was going to fold up on me."

"Well, next time you decide to jump out of a building in a hoop skirt, would you put on a pair of shorts underneath instead of a thong? I didn't appreciate seeing your bare butt as it drifted down to earth."

Gina paused, her expression thoughtful, as if she was actually weighing the pros and cons of my request. Finally, she let out a dramatic sigh. "Fine," she conceded.

We had just reached the parking lot when Darth Vader's deep, echoing voice rang out. I sighed while Gina grinned. Clearly delighted that it wasn't her phone ringing since this particular ringtone was dedicated to one person. Fishing my phone out of my pocket, I felt a familiar sense of exasperation.

"Hi," I said, trying to sound cheerful.

"Sydney, is that you?"

I closed my eyes and sighed. "You know it's me, Mom. You dialed my number."

"It's been so long since I've heard from you; it was hard to tell."

Ah, the classic guilt trip. It was almost a tradition by now every time my mother called.

"Sean's working late tonight," she continued. "Krista is coming over for dinner, and I expect you and Gina to join us."

Initially, my gut reaction was to decline. Each visit with my mother seemed to revolve around her relentless inquiries into my marital status, or rather, the glaring absence of it. I remembered the last time I spent an evening at her house when she had invited a man in an effort to play matchmaker, and the night had turned painfully awkward. Over the last couple of months, I had thrown out countless phone numbers of her friends' single sons because that was never going to happen.

Then I thought about Krista. If we attended the dinner together, perhaps she'd feel compelled to talk with me. Maybe we could finally sort through some of our unresolved issues. Despite the evil eye Gina gave me, I said yes.

"Excellent, I'll see you at six," Mom chirped happily before hanging up.

"I don't know why you always have to drag me along," Gina grumbled.

"You could use a good home-cooked meal," I shot back. "And God knows we aren't going to cook it ourselves." I swung my leg on my motorcycle and straddled the seat. "Besides, it allows you to bond with your favorite sister-in-law."

With a twist of the key, the motorcycle roared to life, drowning out Gina's retort. I shot her a cheeky smile before donning my helmet. In response, she raised her thumb and forefinger, forming an exaggerated 'L' against her forehead.

Revving the throttle, I shot out onto the street, feeling the rush of wind and the thrill of freedom, leaving behind the weight of family expectations.

* * * *

Several hours later, we were heading out of town when the deep, resonant toll of the church bell echoed through the evening air.

"It's really loud," I remarked.

"What?" Gina replied.

I paused, allowing the bell to finish its six chimes.

"What time of night does the bell stop?" I asked.

"I heard the last chime of the day is at ten."

"That seems rather late."

"They wanted it to be authentic. I guess that's when it used to stop back in the day."

As we drove, my eyes were drawn to a curious new device perched on the middle of her dash. It was a small black box. Just as I was about to inquire about it, the red light on the front flickered and turned green.

Amidst the static in the background, a voice crackled through the device, "Farmer Kline's cows broke out and are blocking Solomon Road again. Need assistance."

"Is that a police radio?" I asked.

Gina nodded happily. "Isn't it great? Now we're in the loop about what the cops are doing and where they are. This will give us a real edge while sneaking around during our investigations."

"You mean breaking the law?"

"Call it what you like," she shrugged. "I prefer to think of it as delving into matters."

"Where on earth did you get this? I'm pretty sure this device isn't readily available to the general public."

"I didn't steal it if that's what you're implying," she retorted. "Although that option would have been cheaper. I bought it from my source."

"Uh-huh," I commented, not entirely convinced about the legitimacy of her purchase. "I thought American police scanners were encrypted to keep the conversations private?"

"They are," Gina replied with a mischievous glint in her eye. "Dominic decoded this one for me. It only took him a day to crack the code."

"That boy is going to get himself in trouble one of these days," I said.

Suddenly, the radio crackled to life. "All clear," it announced. "The cows have moo...ved on."

As we parked in the driveway, I noticed a coal-black Dodge Durango with heavily tinted windows parked beside us.

Hesitation set in as I questioned, "Who's SUV is that?"

Gina shrugged, responding that she didn't recognize it.

I felt a knot form in my stomach, fearing that my mother might have invited yet another random suitor to dinner. If that was the case, I was ready to leave. Just then, the driver's door swung open, and Pap stepped out. Relief washed over me as I exited the car.

"What do you think of my new ride?" he announced proudly.

The vehicle was entirely jet black, from the body to the grille, even the wheel rims.

"It doesn't look like your style," I admitted.

Our family's old barn had been transformed into an automotive garage, where my father and grandfather specialized in antique and high-end cars. I couldn't recall ever seeing Pap drive any vehicle made after nineteen seventy.

"This vehicle here is special," he said, an unmistakable excitement in his voice. "Come over here, and I'll show you."

As he swung the door open, I was greeted by a luxurious interior. The plush leather seats promised both comfort and elegance. However, aside from that, the rest of the car was rather unassuming. The entire interior was black with a chrome finish.

"I don't see what's so special," Gina remarked as she rounded her Mustang and joined us.

"I didn't open the door for you to peek inside. I opened it for you to look at the door itself."

My eyebrow shot up as I looked at the side of the door. The exterior paneling was astonishingly thick—at least three times that of a regular car.

"Is this door bulletproof?" I asked, tracing my finger along the cold metal edge of the door.

Pap nodded excitedly. "The entire car is fortified with military-grade armor, and even the windows are bulletproof."

"Where did you get it?" Gina asked.

"Senator Ratcliffe upgraded to one like the president's Cadillac. His new one can withstand a bombing," he replied, kicking the tire. "Can you believe these are Kevlar-reinforced tires? They're shred and puncture resistant. And even if you end up with a flat, it's equipped with steel rims that ensure you can keep driving without missing a beat."

He walked to the front of the vehicle and popped the hood. "It has a hemi supercharged engine with over seven hundred horsepower. It goes from zero to sixty in just over four seconds."

My jaw dropped open in disbelief. "Why do you need a bulletproof rocket-powered SUV?"

He shrugged. "Why not?"

Sadly, I couldn't argue with that logic, considering I would think the same thing.

"And the senator just gave you this vehicle?" Gina asked.

My grandfather, a retired Colonel, had forged numerous connections during his time in the army, and this was one of the perks of his service. "It's not like the government can just auction it off," he replied. "Ratcliffe thought I might have a little fun with it. I'm even considering taking it out to the field later with my shotgun to test how bulletproof it really is."

"Stop flapping your gums and get in here before dinner gets cold," mom yelled through the screen door.

My parents resided in an old stone farmhouse, a steadfast structure that had endured the trials of time. As Pap held the creaky screen door open for us, I could hear the familiar groan of its hinges. My parents took great pride in the rustic charm of their home, avoiding modern updates.

The open wooden ceiling rafters were one of my favorite parts of the old house. They made the rooms look larger and more open. I also fondly remember the brownstone fireplace in the main room. The stones felt cold to the touch no matter the room's temperature. During my childhood, I spent countless evenings curled up in front of its warm, crackling fire.

Dinner awaited us on the table, its enticing aroma wafting through the air as we entered the warmly lit dining room. The feast consisted of crispy fried chicken, mashed potatoes slathered in gravy, and fluffy biscuits. This was Gina's favorite meal.

Gina visibly tensed while I relaxed. My mother had a peculiar habit of preparing someone's favorite meal whenever she wanted something from them, or in my case, when she was on the hunt for a suitable husband for me. Hopefully, since she cooked Gina's favorite meal, she would be badgering her over dinner instead of me.

"Shouldn't we wait for Krista before we start?" I asked as I slid into my seat.

"She's not going to make it tonight," my mother replied. "She has a headache."

I glanced at Gina.

"Did she know we were going to be here?" I couldn't help but ask.

"I told her this afternoon. She called an hour ago to cancel because of the headache."

I guess she wasn't ready to talk to me just yet.

Dad said the prayer, and then we began passing the dishes around the table. Surprisingly, dinner turned out to be enjoyable. Pap and Dad talked about cars, while my mother never once brought up my disappointing life choices. For once, the evening felt relaxed, a brief respite from the usual tension surrounding family dinners.

After dinner, my mother brought out a luscious cheesecake for dessert. Knowing it was my favorite treat, a sense of unease began to wash over me. As my mother expertly sliced the cake into perfect wedges, I decided it was time to confront whatever she was plotting.

"What do you want?" I asked my mother.

"What do you mean," she replied innocently as she slid a generous slice of cheesecake onto a plate and placed it in front of me.

"You invited us to dinner, or more appropriately, ordered us to come and then cook Gina's favorite meal and my favorite dessert," I pressed.

"You want something," Gina chimed in.

"Fine," my mother said passing plates of dessert out to everyone. "The historic committee needs a few more women to play parts in the upcoming reenactment," she finally confessed.

The cheesecake sat tantalizingly on my plate, yet I hadn't even picked up my fork. I loathed the idea of indulging in dessert while being burdened by guilt.

"No," I declare. "I'm not wasting an entire day of my life dressing up in dusty, smelly clothes to parade around a battlefield during the hottest part of summer."

"They don't need anyone for the big battle day. They have enough volunteers for that. What they need are a few volunteers for the impromptu town battles."

"Not good for me. I'll be working," Gina said.

"I'll be helping her," I replied.

"Bull, I haven't even told you when it is," mom interjected. "Show some family pride. The Hayes family has taken part in this reenactment for decades. At least think about it."

"Fine, I'll think about it," I said reluctantly. For all of two seconds. I was already done thinking about it by the time I took my first bite of cheesecake. The creamy texture melted in my mouth, and I couldn't help but sigh contentedly.

My mother chimed in happily. "Doris Prosser told me that she saw you with Chase Mathis downtown today."

What a way to ruin a blissful moment. "So?" I replied before shoveling the next bite into my mouth.

"I heard his parents still live in town. Maybe I'll give his mother a call, and we can all get together for lunch next Sunday," she continued.

I struggled to swallow my bite, feeling like it had turned to lead in my mouth. A gulp of water was necessary to wash it down.

"I'm not dating Chase," I insisted. "I merely said hi to an old friend."

As usual, my mother ignored my protest. "I hear he's still single," she said, looking off dreamily as if she was already planning our wedding.

"And as gorgeous as ever," Gina added.

I kicked Gina under the table, and she bolted up in her seat. I shot her my 'I need to get out of here' look. She fished her phone out of her purse, which was sitting on the table beside her.

"We've got to go," she said urgently, looking at her screen. "Just got a lead on a case."

Without hesitation, she tossed her phone back into her purse, the sound of it thudding against something metal causing her to wince. Since her purse didn't explode, I assumed we were good.

"I didn't even hear it ring," Mom said.

"It's on vibrate," Gina replied.

Mom turned her gaze to the window, the fading light of dusk creeping in. "It's almost dark. What could you possibly be doing at this hour?"

"Chasing an adulterer."

"Following up on a lost dog."

We both replied at once as we sprang from our chairs.

Mom arched an eyebrow.

"Poor woman," Gina said. "She lost her dog last week and now she suspects her husband is cheating on her."

We quickly said goodbye and headed out the door.

Just as we had rolled out of the driveway, the sudden crackle of the police radio shattered the quiet.

"Shots fired!" a voice screamed over the airwaves.

Immediately after a woman's voice cut in calm yet urgent. "Copy, shots fired. All units respond to Faukner Hardware, fifteen Grant Street."

My blood ran cold, while I felt sweat beads form on my forehead. "Did that first voice sound like Sean to you?"

Gina's brow furrowed deeply, her expression tightening with worry as she nodded. "Your mom did mention he was working late tonight."

"Can we make it there?" I asked anxiously.

"Depends on how fast I drive," Gina replied.

"Get us there," I urged as I fastened my seatbelt, my mind a whirlwind of worry about the unfolding crisis ahead.

CHAPTER 3

My seatbelt had barely clicked into place when Gina stepped on the pedal, and my head slammed against the back of the seat.

The vehicle shot forward like a bullet, racing up the hill with breathtaking speed. We soared so high that the wheels barely grazed the ground. As we launched into the air, my head collided with the roof. It felt like I was on a roller coaster ride, and I silently prayed we would make it to the hardware store in one piece.

The trees lining the roadside whipped by in a blur of browns and greens, merging into a colorful haze. Just a glimpse of a sharp bend in the road caught my eye, and I instinctively grasped the overhead "Oh my God" bar, bracing myself. As we careened around the curve on two wheels, an Amish horse and buggy suddenly loomed ahead. The buggy was black, but the bright orange triangle on its rear stood out like a beacon.

"Oh fudge," Gina barely managed to say as she jerked the steering wheel to the left. We narrowly escaped a collision. The speeding car startled the horse, which reared back and bolted down the side of the road in a frenzy. It was a chaotic scene as the carriage wheel tipped precariously off the road, sending it crashing onto its side in the ditch. Driven by fear, the horse didn't even slow down; it just kept running.

With a quick glance in her rearview mirror, Gina muttered, "I'm sure they're fine. We'll check on them later," her voice steady and unfazed as she pressed down harder on the gas.

Gina swerved sharply, cutting off an unmarked black patrol car as we screeched into the dimly lit hardware store parking lot. Two vehicles were in the parking lot, but no one was in site. Gina slammed to a stop next to the white patrol car, causing my seatbelt to lock tight around me, almost choking me with its grip. The pain from my injuries coiled in my chest, but I ignored it as I struggled against the restraint, and as soon as I was free, I bolted from the car.

"What do you think you're doing here?" I heard Blake's voice call out behind me as I rounded the corner of the patrol car.

I halted in my tracks, my breath catching in my throat. Sean was lying on the ground next to the car. I only paused a nanosecond before I ran to his side. Even in the dimly lit parking lot, I could see the crimson blood expanding across his chest.

"No," I whispered, my voice barely audible as I sank to the ground beside him. I pressed two fingers against the side of his neck, straining to find a pulse.

"You shouldn't be h ..." Blake started, his voice faltering as his gaze landed on Sean. His expression shifted, a mix of fear and determination crossed his face as he fished a radio from his pocket. "I need an ambulance now!" He shouted into the device. He hurried over to kneel across from me.

"He has a pulse, but it's thready," I said.

Blake stretched out his hand, palm hovering inches above his mouth, gaze fixed on Sean's still form. "He's breathing," he said with relief.

As I reached for my pocketknife, Blake's eyes widened but he remained silent. The blade snapped open with a sharp click that cut through the air. I grabbed the collar of Sean's shirt and slit it open right down the middle. Just then, Gina rushed to my side, her face pale but focused as she carried a first aid kit.

"He's been shot," I said as I spotted the hole in his upper chest that was slowly gushing dark red blood.

Gina swiftly handed me some gauze pads from the medical kit, and I pressed them against the wound. In a matter of seconds, the dressing was soaked with the warm fluid of life, and so were my hands.

"There's no more gauze in the kit," Gina said, her voice edged with panic.

Blake quickly stripped off his crisp white t-shirt and handed it to me. I wasted no time, using the fabric to reinforce the dressing, ensuring it held tight against Sean's injury. Leaning over him, I bore down with all my weight to stop the relentless flow of blood.

"Sean, stay with us," Gina urged, but there was no response—only the sound of ragged breaths and the distant wail of sirens.

Tears welled up in my eyes as I silently prayed the ambulance would arrive here in time. Each moment felt like an eternity, but it was merely minutes before a paramedic tapped my shoulder with a firm hand.

"We'll take it from here," he said.

I stepped back, my heart pounding, as they moved in to assess Sean's condition. Gina wrapped her arm around my shoulder, offering a fragile sense of comfort.

"It's going to be okay," she whispered, though uncertainty hung thick in the air.

Another person burst forth from the ambulance, urgently pulling a stretcher that rattled and squeaked, its wheels wobbling awkwardly as they scraped across the pavement. As I observed the frantic scene unfolding before me, I finally allowed my gaze to wander, and for the first time, I noticed several other officers standing nearby. The glare of red and blue lights flickered from two additional patrol cars parked in the lot. I had been so engrossed in the moment that I hadn't even registered their arrival.

"Why don't you call Krista and take her to the hospital?" Blake suggested.

I shook my head firmly, shaking off my panic and reminding myself to remain the level-headed person I prided myself on being.

"He's my brother-in-law. I'm not leaving," I said.

"I'll call Krista and our parents," Gina said as she walked away.

Blake let out a sigh. "You need to move away from the crime scene. Go over there," he instructed, pointing to the other side of the lot.

Reluctantly, I complied, but I ensured Sean remained within my line of sight.

I repeatedly dragged my hands down the fabric of my shorts, hoping to wipe away the thick blood that clung to me. It was almost futile. I found myself leaning against the cool metal of the other car parked in the lot.

"He certainly looks good without a shirt on," Gina remarked, attempting to lighten the atmosphere.

I stole a glance at Blake as he stood there, the dark fabric of a new shirt draped over one arm, ready to be pulled on. With his arms stretched above his head, he showcased a physique that screamed athlete. His sculpted muscles were chiseled while his washboard abs caught the dim light. I quickly diverted my attention back to Sean, trying to shake off the momentary distraction.

Pushing off the car, I began to pace which was my usual response to frustration and worry. The repetitive movement helped clear my mind, a grounding ritual of sorts. As I passed the back corner of the vehicle, illuminated only by the faint glow overhead, something caught my eye. There was a shimmer of liquid beneath the bumper. I found this odd since it hadn't rained in a week.

Kneeling down for a closer look, I observed a dark puddle of liquid mimicking the color of the asphalt in this poor lighting. I put two fingers in the liquid and ran my thumb against them. The substance felt oddly thick against my skin. Straightening up, I fished my phone from my pocket and flicked on the flashlight. My fingers were once again covered in a deep red liquid.

"Where did you get fresh blood from?" Gina asked as she glanced over my shoulder.

"Hold this," I said, handing my phone to Gina. As I reached down to retrieve the lockpicks from my boot, she directed the light from my phone onto the trunk of the gray sedan.

"There's no lock," she exclaimed.

I couldn't help but smile at her reaction. "A lot of newer cars skip the traditional lock. You either pull the latch from inside the car or use your key fob," I explained.

"This is exactly why I drive a classic," Gina replied as we approached the driver's door. Gina shined the light on the lock, but before I used my lockpicks, I decided to try the handle. To my surprise, it opened effortlessly.

"Takes all the thrill out of breaking in when the door's unlocked," Gina remarked.

I leaned in and, with a satisfying thunk, popped the trunk open. My gaze flickered over to the scene unfolding nearby, where paramedics were loading Sean onto a gurney and maneuvering him into the back of the ambulance. Meanwhile, Blake stood commanding the scene, his voice barking orders to the other two officers. Noone was paying us any attention.

I lifted the trunk lid while Gina shown the light in. To our surprise, there was the body of a dead man stuffed inside. He looked of Middle Eastern descent, and his eyes were fixed with an expression of shock.

Gina handed me a pair of latex gloves.

"Take a few pictures," I said as I donned the gloves. After Gina took a few pictures, I leaned in and pulled the blue shirt away from the body.

"A little more light, please," I said

Gina leaned the phone in closer, and I could see two circular holes in the middle of his chest.

"Looks like he was shot," I said. "Shine the light around the trunk and see if there is anything else inside."

Gina directed the light around the edges of the trunk, but it was empty except for the body.

"I have a question," Gina said. "If he was shot in the middle of the chest and is lying on his right side, why is the left side of his chest covered in blood?"

"He was probably shot first and then shoved in the trunk," I said, but I lifted his left arm up to verify there were no other wounds.

My eyes opened wide when I looked at his arm. The skin was completely missing from the inside of his upper left arm. The wound was so clean and precise; It looked like the skin had been sliced off with a knife.

"Who takes the skin off the arm of a dead guy?" Gina asked as she took a picture of his arm with my phone.

"You don't want to know, and honestly, I'd rather not dwell on it right now," I muttered, lowering the arm back down over the lifeless body tucked away in the trunk. I peeled off the gloves and stuffed them into my pocket.

I turned to call for Blake but my voice was lost amidst the chaos surrounding us.

Gina put two fingers in her mouth and unleashed a sharp, piercing whistle. It cut through the air like a knife, instantly silencing the clamor and drawing every pair of eyes to us. In the distance, I heard a chorus of dogs barking in response.

"Could you please warn me before you do that again?" I complained, my ears buzzing from the sudden noise.

I shouted, directing my voice at a clearly annoyed Blake. "You need to see something."

He made his way over, curiosity breaking through his annoyance as he approached the trunk. The moment he glanced inside, his face went pale.

"Christ," he breathed, running his hand through his disheveled hair.

His eyes locked onto mine. "How did you know there was a body in the trunk?"

I sighed. "Because cars don't bleed."

CHAPTER 4

We approached the desk inside the double glass doors of the emergency room, the hum of medical chatter seemed all around us. A middle-aged woman sat behind the counter, her thick-rimmed glasses low on her nose, which was adorned with a gold beaded chain that draped around her neck. She was engrossed in a romance novel, oblivious to the world surrounding her.

"We're here to see Sean Wallace," I said impatiently.

Without lifting her gaze from the pages, she replied, "Are you family or friend?"

"Family," Gina replied.

At last, her cynical eyes flicked up from the book, surveying us with mild disinterest. "His family is already here," she stated flatly, her focus drifting back to her novel.

I leaned over the desk and snatched the book from her hands to get her full attention. "You need to tell us where 'the family,'" I said, air quotes punctuating my irritation, "is before you become a patient in the ER yourself."

Her expression transformed into one of surprise, and a hint of fear flickered in her eyes. "In the waiting room down the hall on your left," she stammered.

I placed the book on the desk as I turned to head down the corridor, while Gina murmured her thanks the woman.

As I stepped into the waiting room, I saw my entire family already gathered. A man in a long white lab coat was speaking softly to Krista. I assumed he was the doctor.

"Your husband was lucky in one respect," the doctor announced. "The bullet struck high enough in the chest to miss all his vital organs. He'll require surgery to remove the bullet, but it's a minimal procedure."

A wave of relief washed over Krista, her shoulders lightening as she inhaled.

"You said in one respect?" my mother questioned as she stood beside Krista. Behind them, my father and Pap hovered, their faces cloaked in worry.

The doctor's expression turned serious, his frown deepened. "When he fell, he hit the back of his head, jarring his brain. A CT scan showed swelling in the brain. That's most likely why he was unconscious upon arrival."

At this, Krista's tears began to flow, her body trembling as she absorbed the gravity of the news. My mom wrapped her arm around her shoulder.

"A concussion of this caliber can be serious," the doctor continued. "He's on his way to the operating room now. I'll keep you updated on his progress." With a nod of his head, he turned and walked through the heavy metal door behind him.

Dad and Pap settled into their chairs, making themselves comfortable for what promised to be a long wait.

I approached Krista from behind. "What can I do?" I asked, trying to offer my support.

She spun around abruptly, her tear-stained face instantly morphing from sorrow to anger. "What are you doing here?" The intensity of her voice escalated with each word, sharp and insistent. "You need to leave. I don't want you here." Her foot stomped against the floor like a thunderclap, and she turned away.

Gina stepped forward, placing a reassuring hand on my shoulder. "Why don't we grab coffee for everyone?" she suggested.

With that, she guided me out of the room and down the hallway. We followed the cafeteria signs down the dimly lit hallway. The late hour cast an eerie atmosphere; the silence was punctuated only by the distant hum of unfamiliar machines hidden behind closed doors.

Upon reaching the cafeteria, we discovered it was closed for the night, its lights dark and forbidding. Just then, an employee clad in navy scrubs emerged through a door adjacent to the cafeteria, a steaming cup of coffee in one hand and a crinkly bag of chips in the other. We inquired about the source of her coffee. She informed us that there were vending machines located in the basement.

With newfound purpose, Gina opened the door leading to the stairwell and bounded down the stairs. By the time I reached the bottom and pushed through the door, she was already disappearing around a corner. I quickened my pace and caught up to her just outside two imposing double doors. One door bore a large, orange triangular sign that blared 'Biohazard,' while the other displayed a similarly foreboding sign reading "Authorized Personnel Only.'

"I bet this is the morgue," Gina said, her eyes sparkling with a mix of curiosity and excitement as she peered at the heavy doors.

"Haven't you seen enough of the inside of morgues lately?"

Several weeks ago, we had spent way too much time in a morgue. The case we were working on resulted in more dead bodies than Jack the Ripper produced.

"I want to see inside," she insisted.

"You're weird," I said, shaking my head, half-amused.

She grabbed the handle. "Most people fawn over the newborn baby ward. You can keep the babies, I want the real stories."

"And if we get caught?"

"We were looking for the vending machine and took a wrong turn."

"In the morgue?"

"We didn't know it was the morgue," she protested, gesturing at the door. "There's no sign stating it's the morgue."

She pulled the door open, stepping inside without hesitation.

"You'd think they would keep the door to the morgue locked," I said.

"I know, right? Go figure," she replied, stepping further into the brightly lit room.

The harsh glare of fluorescent lights greeted us. The air smelled like a mixture of antiseptic and vinegar. In the center of the room stood a solitary stretcher, its metallic frame stark against the sterile floor. It was draped with a body-shaped black canvas.

"Oh goody, there's a body," Gina exclaimed.

"They write horror books about people like you," I replied. "But seriously, why are all the lights on?"

"Because the funeral home is coming to pick up the body," came a response from down the hall to my left, just as Rocco Salvino came into view.

Gina was so startled that when she pivoted, her foot snagged on the leg of the stretcher. In a frantic attempt to regain her balance, she reached for the gurney, but her grip faltered, pushing the gurney forward with surprising speed.

It was as if the wheels had been recently lubricated as it raced toward Rocco, who leapt back to get out of the way. It zipped past him like a runaway freight train.

The doors at the end of the corridor were wide open, looking out onto a ramp. The gurney hit the ramp and picked up speed as it careened downward, barreling towards the parking lot. Rocco and I sprinted after it, but we were too late. It crashed into the side of a white Cadilac.

The impact sent the gurney tumbling onto its side, spilling the body onto the rough pavement. The black tarp that had concealed it was thrown aside, revealing a black body bag underneath. The body bag blended seamlessly with the dark pavement and was unseen by the car speeding recklessly toward it. The vehicle bumped over it without a hint of hesitation.

In shock, I clamped a hand over my mouth while Rocco, who was always pale as a ghost, turned an even grayer shade. The car came to a halt, and a security officer jumped out. When he saw what he had run over, his face drained of color, I thought he was going to pass out. Everyone stood silent for a moment not quit sure how to process the scene that just unfolded.

Rocco strolled over with an air of confidence and effortlessly righted the gurney before picking up the body bag with such little effort that it appeared as if it were light as a feather.

"What's going on here?" the security guard finally asked the color completely drained from his face.

"The gurney got away from me," Rocco said, glancing at Gina and giving her a wink.

"Who are they?" the guard asked, directing the beam of his flashlight towards Gina and me. The flashlight was a bit of an overkill since the parking lot was lit up like a runway.

"I was giving them directions to the emergency room," Rocco explained.

The security guard's gaze flickered back to the body. "I ran over a dead person," he stated, wringing his hands anxiously. "How am I supposed to write up this report? I'm going to get fired."

I couldn't help myself, I chuckled. The absurdity of writing a report stating you ran over a dead body already in a body bag wasn't lost on me. I was not even sure his superiors would believe him.

"Don't write it up," Rocco said. "Mr. Nicholes is scheduled to get cremated in the morning. No one needs to know about this."

"What about the dent in the car it hit?" the guard protested, his flashlight illuminating a noticeable indentation in the middle of the door.

I scanned the vicinity, noticing the absence of security cameras around the building. "There's no cameras in the parking lot?"

He shook his head.

I was astonished by the lack of surveillance in small towns. In cities, even in Italy, most establishments had cameras to monitor potential criminal activities.

"I didn't see anything," I said. "Did you?"

Gina and Rocco both shook their heads. The security officer paused, weighing his options. Without another word he slipped back into his car and drove off at a much slower pace.

"Always an adventure with you two," Rocco remarked with a grin as he pushed the gurney towards the hearse.

"I'm starving," Gina declared. "Let's find those vending machines."

We found the vending machines and carried our steaming cups of coffee and bags of chips back to the waiting room. When we entered, Krista and Mom were gone, leaving only Pap and Dad.

"Where did the other two go?" I asked, handing Dad a styrofoam cup of coffee.

"The nurse came out and told Krista she could wait in the patient room they had prepared for Sean. Your mother went with her," Dad said.

We settled into our seats, the plastic chair creaking softly beneath me. I sipped my coffee, but truth be told, I didn't need it to keep me awake. Stressful situations always made my adrenaline run high, making me feel wired and alert. After an hour of anxiously waiting, my mom finally emerged through the door.

Her expression was fraught with worry, exhaustion etched lines into her face. She sank into the chair next to Dad, who grasped her hand in his.

"Sean's out of surgery," she announced. "The doctor said it went well, but he's still concerned about the concussion. Sean will sleep the rest of the night from the anesthesia and will be re-evaluated in the morning."

"What about his parents?" Gina asked.

"They're on vacation in Aruba," Mom replied. "They don't know when they'll be able to catch a flight back."

"Why don't you all go home tonight and get some sleep," I suggested. "I'll stay here in case Krista needs me."

My mother opened her mouth to protest, but my father gently squeezed her hand. "Anita, it's best if you get some rest tonight so you can be here for Krista tomorrow."

Resigned, Mom nodded, and together, they rose to leave.

"Are you sure?" Gina asked, her voice dropping to a whisper as she leaned towards me. "She may not want you here."

I shrugged. "Then she'll have to get over it. Sean's my family too."

The waiting room chairs with their vinyl upholstery in a dull shade of dark grey, were the standard straight-back type, complete with black plastic armrests. At least the seats were padded, providing some minuscule amount of comfort. I leaned my head against the cold wall, trying to find a semblance of relaxation, and settled in for a long night.

My thoughts drifted to the stiff in the trunk. Why was that man there, and who shot him? The absence of skin from his arm replayed in my mind and was my biggest concern. He just couldn't be who I feared he was.

At some point, exhaustion claimed me, pulling me into an uneasy sleep. I was jolted awake by the swishing sound of the door opening. I was trained to react to the slightest noise and normally would have leaped to my feet and instinctively reached for my weapon, but the awkward position I had fallen asleep in left me stiff and sore.

Krista stood in the doorway. Her gaze was fixed on me with an unreadable expression. Slowly, I stood up and stretched my arms above my head attempting to loosen the tightness in my muscles after the less-than-stellar sleeping arrangement.

Krista tilted her head slightly, studying me. "You're still here?" she asked, her tone neutral, lacking the venom that had colored her words during our last encounter.

I nodded. "You're my sister."

"And the others?"

"They'll be back in the morning."

"It is morning," she said.

I looked out the window and saw the sun rising over the jagged mountain peaks. The sky transformed into a picture-perfect orange and purple palette. Returning my gaze to Krista, I could see the morning light illuminating her features and casting gentle shadows across her expression.

"Come with me," she said.

I followed her through the door and down the corridor. The ceiling lights were all on now, their bright fluorescent glow reflecting off the stark white wall, giving the sterile environment a clinical feel. The air smelled like a mixture of blood and ammonia.

We entered a room where Sean lay in a hospital bed with his eyes closed. He appeared ghostly pale. In stark contrast was the angry red bruise on his left cheek.

"Has he woken up?" I asked.

She shook her head, her sadness showing in her eyes. "Please sit down."

I settled into the chair positioned at the far end of the room. Krista pushed a chair from the side of the bed over, its feet scraping against the linoleum floor. She sat down facing me.

We sat in silence for several moments, each of us grappling with the unspoken words that hung heavy in the air.

"I'm so sorry," she finally broke the silence, tears welling up in her eyes.

I straightened in my chair.

"What could you possibly be sorry for?" I asked.

"For being mad at you," she replied, her voice trembling. "I should have been happy you had a job you loved and were proud to do."

"No," I said, shaking my head. "I'm sorry for lying to you all those years. You're my sister and I owed you the truth."

"I understand now why you kept it from me," she replied, casting a glance at Sean, who lay motionless on the bed. "Spending all night here with him helped put things into perspective for me." She turned her gaze back to me. "I would have constantly worried about you if I'd known." A smile creased her lips. "I would have called you every day just to make sure you were still alive. I would have driven you crazy."

I leaned forward and gave her a hug. "Don't worry, your aunt's going to drive me crazy first. So, we're good?"

She nodded.

I glanced over at Sean lying in bed. He was hooked up to wires and tubes, including a monitor that beeped rhythmically. The screen displayed the jagged wave of his heartbeat while an IV drip hung beside him.

"I'm sorry about Sean," I said. "Gina and I did everything we could to get to him in time, but it was too late."

She looked at me, confusion etched on her face. "How did you find out about the shooting?"

I recounted our frantic drive, the newly acquired police radio, and Gina's wild imagination as she thought her car was a jet engine while we sped toward the scene.

"I'm surprised you're still alive," she said, giggling when I got to the part about the overturned Amish buggy.

"So am I. Just let me know if there's anything I can do for you. Do you need me to go to your house to get anything?"

"No," she said, her face growing serious once more. "But there is something you can do for me."

"Name it."

"Now that I know what you really do for a living, I can only think of one thing. Find the bastard who shot my husband." Krista's voice was laced with seething anger that cut through the quiet room.

I nodded. "You know I will."

She reached into her pocket and retrieved her car keys, which she handed to me to drive home. As I rose and made my way towards the door, the atmosphere shifted abruptly.

Two men strode into the room, their presence commanding and brimming with arrogance. Both had firearms holstered to their hips and badges clipped to their belts. They cast a fleeting glance at Sean, still sleeping peacefully, then turned their attention to us.

"Mrs. Wallace?" the first officer inquired, his tone formal yet edged with impatience.

"That's me," Krista said, rising from her chair.

"We would like to speak to you," he said with an unmistakable furrow forming on his brow as he glanced at me, a silent signal suggesting that I should exit.

With a defiant smile, I plopped back down in my chair letting him know that I had no intention of leaving.

"And you are?" Officer One asked with irritation lacing his voice.

"She's my sister," Krista replied. "And I'd like her to stay."

I stifled the urge to flash him a smug smile. He barely acknowledged me, his eyes narrowing as he pressed on.

"Your husband was working the late shift yesterday?" Officer One continued.

"Yes," Krista replied. "His shift was to end at midnight."

"Did he frequently work late shifts?"

"Maybe once a week. More if they are short-staffed," Krista answered.

"Was it always the same day of the week?"

"No, it varied," Krista replied, her brow furrowing in confusion. I could see the wheels turning in her mind, and we were both grappling with the relevance of these relentless questions.

Officer One flicked a glance at Officer Two, who stood rigid against the wall, nodding subtly in response.

"Has your husband been acting differently at home? Maybe taking more phone calls or spending more time away?"

I jumped out of my chair. "Who are you?" I demanded.

Officer One's jaw tightened visibly, and I could tell he was irked by my interruption. "I was addressing Mrs. Wallace."

"I'm aware," I shot back. "I'm also aware that you're questioning her as if her husband is a suspect rather than a victim."

"We're trying to ascertain what happened last night," Officer One said.

"And you also didn't answer my question. She has a right to know who she is addressing," I insisted.

Officer One's expression hardened, and I was sure he was on the verge of throwing me out of the room.

"They're state police troopers," Blake announced as he stepped into the room. "These are Trooper Rhode and Trooper Grant.

Officer Rhode adjusted his stance, a subtle show of authority, as he declared, "We are in charge of this case."

I glanced at Blake, who shook his head and shrugged.

"That's fine," I replied, crossing my arms over my chest. "But if you intend to pursue this line of questioning, I will encourage my sister to contact her lawyer."

"I can ask your sister any questions I like," Trooper Grant shot back, a smug grin on his face.

At that moment, Krista's shoulders straightened as though a fog of sadness had lifted, and the reality around her began to crystallize. "No, you can't," she said firmly, her voice steady. "I didn't properly introduce myself. Krista Wallace, attorney at law."

Trooper Grant's expression darkened, his glare fierce enough to cut glass, and I could see the tension in his jaw as it tightened. He pulled out a business card with a flourish, handing it to Krista with a curt nod. "When your husband wakes up, call us immediately." He pivoted abruptly to face Blake. "Can we see you outside?"

"What's going on?" Krista asked, a note of anxiety creeping into her voice. "Do they think Sean was at fault somehow?"

"I don't know," I replied. "But I'm going to find out."

As I exited the room, I caught sight of Blake standing further down the hall in a heated discussion with the state troopers. Trooper Rhode's voice rang out as he waged a finger at Blake.

I was already irritated by their treatment of Krista, so I strolled up to them, making an effort to plaster a smile on my face. "Am I interrupting anything?"

Trooper Rhode looked at me as if I was an annoying gnat he wanted to squash. He didn't bother to respond. Instead, he simply turned on his heel and strode off down the hallway, his partner close behind.

"I bet they're a blast at parties," I said as I watched the two officers retreat. "Why are they in charge?"

Blake let out a weary sigh. "A town officer has been shot, we've got a dead body on our hands, and no sheriff. Anytime an officer discharges their weapon, it triggers an investigation, which means an outside agency steps in. The state police swooped right in on this one."

"Do they think Sean shot the guy?" I asked.

Blake shrugged. "They were just making it clear that this is their investigation. They expect me to stay out of their way and not cross any lines."

"Creeps," I said as I turned to leave. Just as I stepped away, Blake stopped me by grabbing my arm.

"You need to back off of this case," he cautioned. "The state police won't be as forgiving as I have been in the past."

"Ha," I laughed, brushing off his hand. "You are hardly lenient. Besides," I continued, "it's Sean we're talking about."

I could hear him sigh as I walked away.

CHAPTER 5

When I arrived at the house, Gina was still nestled under the blankets, her hair a tousled mess, completely oblivious to my presence. I gently shook her shoulder, causing her to bolt upright in bed, eyes wide, confusion etched across her face.

"I didn't do it," she blurted out, still half-asleep.

I chuckled. "Whatever it was, I'm sure you did it."

She stuck her tongue out at me as she stretched her arms above her head. "Give me some time to get ready, and I'll make breakfast."

Before I could respond, the church bell began to chime, alerting us that it was seven o'clock.

"Is that the first chime of the day?" I asked.

"No, it started at six a.m. Can you believe that?"

I shook my head. "I'm going for a quick jog before breakfast." I headed to my room to change. Despite the exhaustion lingering from a restless night, I was committed to my exercise routine. It was the only way I would get back in shape to rejoin my team after my accident. I quickly changed into my workout clothes, lacing my sneakers tightly.

Stepping out onto the sidewalk, I stood for a moment, stretching my tired muscles. The cool morning air brushed against my skin, invigorating my spirit.

"Sydney, how are you?" Jean called out from her front porch. Jean was the senior citizen from across the street. She resided there with her prehistoric mother, Beatrix.

"I'm well. How's your mother?" I asked, bending down to grab my foot and pulling it up behind me in a stretch.

"Not well," Jean replied. "She fell off the back porch yesterday and broke her leg. She's in the hospital now."

At her age, Beatrix's bones were probably as fragile as raw spaghetti noodles.

"I'm heading for my jog," I said, finishing my stretching routine.

"TTYL," Jean replied.

"Excuse me?" I asked as I released my foot.

"My grandkids are trying to teach me texting abbreviations. It means 'Talk to you later.'"

I set off at a slow, deliberate pace, allowing my body to warm up, but soon my spirits surged, and I increased my speed. Each day, I felt stronger, pushing myself to run a few miles every other day. On my off days, I engaged in workouts at the gym above the garage. At this rate, I was confident I would be back to full duty in no time.

As I jogged through the neighborhood, I had to admit it was lovely. The air smelled crisp and fresh with a hint of flowers, and it was peaceful and quiet. Everyone was friendly, and as I passed, neighbors greeted me with a wave and cheerful hellos. It was the best part of small-town life. Living in the city, even in a foreign land, you could look forward to smog and the noises of traffic and commotion. If you weren't careful, you would collide with someone who wouldn't spare you a second glance.

About a block away from the house, I heard some barking, drawing my attention to the yard I had just passed. As I continued my route, I noticed the barking was growing increasingly closer rather than fading into the distance. I turned around to see a Rottweiler charging towards me. It barked and growled with a menacing intensity.

Instinct kicked in, and I took off, sprinting up the driveway and flinging open the gate to the backyard. I was nearly at the screen door when I felt the sudden and fierce tug at the back sole of my sneaker. The dog had latched on, growling and slobbering.

Before I could even consider reaching for my gun, Cagney burst onto the scene, flapping her wings in a wild frenzy and squawking loudly. The dog's attention shifted from me to the chicken, momentarily halting its growl, but it still clutched my shoe.

Cagney flew up into the air and pelted the dog in the face with her feathers while she pecked him repeatedly on the head with her sharp little beak. The startled Rottweiler released my shoe and backed up. Cagney floated back down to the ground beside me. The dog glanced hesitantly between Cagney and me before bolting out of the yard. Guess he didn't think I was worth the wrath of the chicken.

I looked down at my savior. "Thank you," I said.

Cagney regarded me with her beady little eyes for a moment before delivering a surprising Bruce Lee super kick to my leg before waddling away.

Jerk.

I found Gina seated at the wooden kitchen table reading the paper while Dominic bustled around the stove. During my rush to get away from the angry dog, I must have overlooked Dominic's car parked in the driveway. Dominic was my closest friend from school who, for some unknown reason, liked to break in and whip up breakfast. Not that I was about to complain.

"Good morning," I greeted as I slid into a chair beside Gina. I reached for a piece of bacon, which was surprisingly not greasy, and took a bite. It was warm and infused with a smoky flavor, but lacking the fatty taste I was accustomed to.

"What's wrong with the bacon?" I asked, noting its peculiar texture.

"It's turkey bacon," Dominic replied, flipping a golden pancake in the sizzling pan. "It's so much healthier for you."

I wrinkled my nose and dropped it back on the plate.

"You're probably one of the last fifteen people left in town who still subscribe to the newspaper," I said to Gina as I poured myself a steaming cup of coffee from the pot sitting on the table.

"I don't subscribe," Gina replied. "I steal it off my neighbor's porch."

"And your neighbor doesn't mind?"

"I'll return it when I'm done. He'll think the paperboy was late again," she said, the page crinkling as she turned it. "Happenings in Gettysburg this week. Of course, the reenactment and all the activities that accompany it."

I rolled my eyes. "Hard pass."

"Amen sister," Dominic chimed in as he deposited a stack of steaming, fluffy pancakes onto the table. Their sweet scent wafting through the room.

I jumped up to grab the syrup out of the pantry.

"Hum," Gina said. "The Vice President is coming into town this year to give a speech the last evening of the reenactment."

"Big deal," Dominic replied, pouring syrup generously onto his pancakes. "The President himself visited a couple of years ago."

A loud squawk pierced the air, drawing our attention towards the window. There, perched on the sill like a regal sentinel, was Lacey, eyeing Dominic curiously.

"Well, aren't you a pretty bird," he said with a smile.

Lacey puffed up her feathers, swelling with pride at the compliment. He gently stroked her neck, and she responded with soft coos. It felt as though I was the only person the chickens hated.

"Here you go," he said, extending his hand with a piece of bacon. Lacey eagerly plucked it from his fingers before she hopped off the windowsill and strutted away.

"Anything else going on this week?" Dominic inquired just as the church bells began to chime.

The chickens ran around the yard like... well... chickens with their heads cut off, before disappearing into their coop. We paused the conversation as the chiming of the clock filled the air.

"I'm not sure I'll ever get used to that," Gina remarked, glancing back down at the newspaper. "Oh look, the trout derby's coming up next weekend."

"So?" I asked.

"I have a boat now. We should definitely enter."

"You mean that little aluminum thing in your garage?"

She set the newspaper on the table. "It's not exactly the Proud Mary, but it's a perfectly good bass boat. Plus, Mini mentioned Charlie installed a new motor on it shortly before he disappeared."

Mini and Charlie were the previous owners of the house. It seemed Mini had not only left the chickens behind but also the boat when she sold the place to Gina.

"I'll ask Willy to tow it to the docks for me," Gina said, already pulling out her phone to send a quick text to Willy. Her excitement was palpable.

As I took a bite of my fluffy, warm, syrupy pancake, I turned to Dominic, curious about his presence. "What brings you here this morning?" I asked.

"Please, after what happened last night. I assumed you'd be up early poking your nose into yet another police investigation."

"Of course we are," I replied. "But how do you know about last night?"

"Gina's not the only one with a police radio. So, bring me up to speed on what's happening so far."

We filled Dominic in on the scene in the parking lot last night, and then I filled them both in on my run-in with the state police.

"We're going to have to be a bit sneakier this time with the state police involved," Gina said.

"I agree," I said. "Can you run the license plate number on the abandoned vehicle that was in the parking lot?" I asked Dominic.

Dominic nodded.

"Do you still have the number?" I turned to Gina, who had already leapt from the chair.

She ambled over to her large carry-on, which she referred to as a purse, and rummaged through its depths. After a moment of fruitless searching, she began to pull out random items—her wallet clattered to the table, followed by an array of objects: a stick of dynamite, handcuffs, a fork, a bag of birdseed, and a few loose bullets that had obviously been rolling around at the bottom of her purse.

With a playful shrug, she continued her search, unzipping a side pocket and finally producing a small notepad.

"Forgot I tucked it in there," she said, ripping off the top page and handing it to Dominic, who was still trying to process what had been revealed.

"You seemed very interested in the dead guy in the trunk last night," Gina remarked. "Why?"

"It's not sitting well with me," I confessed.

"A car abandoned in a parking lot with a dead guy in the trunk," Dominic said sarcastically. "I can't fathom why that seems odd to you."

I sent him a withering glare while I pulled my phone out of my pocket. I scrolled through my photos until I found the picture I sought, holding my screen out for Gina to see. "Have you ever seen this before?" I asked.

On my phone's screen was the striking image of a tattoo: a silver dagger, its elegantly curved tip piercing a vivid red heart.

She shook her head.

"This tattoo belongs to a terrorist organization known as Tasqhir," I explained.

"What does that mean?" Gina asked.

"To conquer. More fittingly, to conquer with violence."

Dominic leaned back, skepticism etched in his features. "I don't see how this is relevant to Sean's shooting."

I pointed to the inside of my left upper arm, tracing an invisible line where the ink usually resided. "Every member brands the tattoo in the same spot, right here. Close to the heart."

Gina leaned closer to the photograph, her brow furrowing as she took in the unsettling details. "The dead guy in the trunk was missing the skin on that part of his arm. So you think someone cut off a tattoo before he was killed?"

"Or after he was dead," I said. "Either way, it's clear that someone went to great lengths to keep whatever was on that arm hidden from the police. There is a good chance it was a Tasqhir tattoo."

"But why?" Dominic asked.

"To remove suspicion," I said. "If the tattoo remained, and the police pursued it, it would lead straight back to the terrorist organization."

A light flickered in Gina's eyes as she snapped her fingers in realization. "But without the tattoo, local police won't even know these markings exist."

"Precisely," I nodded. "This allows them to carry on with their operations without the threat of interruption from law enforcement."

Dominic leaned in closer. "What's that symbol on the handle?"

"It's Persian for justice."

"Do you really think there are terrorists in town?" Gina asked, her brow furrowed with concern.

I blew out a breath. "I don't know," I admitted. "But the hairs on the back of my neck are standing up and there's a gnawing feeling in my gut that tells me something isn't right."

Gina shook her head. "That's not good," she said, turning to Dominic. "Her gut is never wrong."

"Why would they be here?" Dominic asked.

"I really don't know," I replied, frustration creeping into my tone. "They prefer attacking large cities, like Washington DC or New York. I can't fathom why they'd choose this quiet spot."

Gina chimed in. "We are strategically located between several large cities. DC is less than an hour away."

Dominic nodded, adding his thoughts. "Don't forget Baltimore and Philly. Maybe they're hiding out here, biding their time until they're ready to strike."

"How would Sean get himself involved in something like that?" Gina asked.

"He could have stumbled across them while investigating a case, or perhaps he was simply caught in the wrong place at the wrong time. We won't know for sure until he regains consciousness."

"So what's our next move?" Gina asked.

Suddenly, a gunshot rang out, echoing through the air as if it had been fired a few feet away from us. Gina and I instinctively dropped to the ground and I reached for the gun hidden in the waistband of my shorts. Meanwhile, Dominic remained unmoved, leisurely sipping his coffee as if nothing had happened.

I cautiously crept towards the back door. The screen creaked softly as I nudged it open, a sound that betrayed my efforts to be silent. I couldn't help but grimace. Every single door in Gina's place had that same irritating squeak, a constant reminder that I needed to invest in some oil. Stealth was already a challenge; the last thing I needed was the sound of rusted hinges giving away my presence.

As I peered around the door frame, I spotted an intriguing figure standing ominously beside the neighboring house. He was an elderly man, his face etched with the lines of time, grasping an antique rifle that exhaled wisps of gray smoke from its barrel, creating an eerie atmosphere. The most captivating aspect of his appearance was his attire. A complete navy blue uniform reminiscent of the Civil War. The fabric looked heavy and faded, accompanied by polished black boots that gleamed in the soft morning light and a navy cap perched firmly upon his head. On his hip hung a saber, its blade reflecting the sunlight. The outfit looked so old, I wondered if it was an original piece.

Before I could draw my gun on him, Gina pushed past me and headed out the door looking angry.

"Oliver Chappell," she yelled. "You better not be shooting at my chickens again." With determined strides, she marched right up to him, her eyes blazing with indignation.

"Humph," he grumbled in response.

Gina balled up her fist. "I should punch you in the face."

A black car glided to a stop at the curb, and Blake emerged with a frown etched across his face. "A call came in about shots being fired," he said, his brow furrowed in annoyance. "Why am I not surprised your address was listed?"

"He was the one firing the shots," Gina said, her finger pointing accusatorily at the lunatic clad in the costume. "Arrest him."

"She was going to hit me," Oliver exclaimed.

Blake glanced at me. "Any comments from you?"

I raised my hands. "For once, I have no idea what's going on."

Dominic stood behind me with a wide grin as he raised his phone to snap a picture. "This is great."

"Fine," Blake said, sighing heavily. "Gina, give me your version of the story."

Gina squared her shoulders. "He tried to shoot my chickens. Again."

"Those pesky chickens keep wandering onto my property," Oscar exclaimed.

"No they don't," Gina retorted.

"They perch on top of the fence over there," Oliver pointed his finger towards the wooden boundary that marked his yard. "When they do half of them hangs over the property line."

"And that's a problem?" Blake asked.

"Darn right," Oliver said. "They always hang their behinds over my side of the fence and poop all over my meticulously kept yard." He proceeded to scratch his butt absentmindedly. "Stupid wool uniforms," he muttered.

"You really can't make this crap up," Dominic whispered in my ear mimicking my thoughts.

"Mr. Chappel," Blake said, rubbing his temple. He was probably wishing he hadn't taken the call. "You can't fire a gun inside town limits. Furthermore, you're not permitted to shoot your neighbor's pets."

"Chickens aren't pets. They're dinner," Mr. Chappel retorted with a smirk.

Gina puffed up. "Can you arrest him?"

Blake shook his head. "But I can fine him for unlawful discharge of a firearm."

"It's reenactment week," Oliver said smugly. "Plenty of people are going to be firing guns around here."

"Are there live rounds in yours?" Blake inquired.

Oliver was silent, though the tips of his ears flushed an unmistakable shade of pink, betraying him.

Blake took a deep breath. "Now, everyone go back into your own houses," he commanded.

With a dramatic flair, Oliver pivoted on one foot, mimicking a soldier, before striding back toward his front door.

"Stay away from my chickens!" Gina shouted after him.

Blake tipped his head towards us before returning to his car.

Dominic shook his head and with a chuckle, heading to his own vehicle. "Never a dull moment," he murmured as he went.

"What's on the agenda for today?" I asked Gina.

"Keeping an eye out for anyone suspicious," Gina suggested. "We can stroll through town and see if anyone seems to stand out."

I raised an eyebrow, skepticism etched on my face. "It's tourist season. Honestly, everyone here looks like they've wandered in from a different world. Besides you know how much I hate the crowds during this time of year."

Gina shrugged. "It's the only lead I can come up with at the moment."

"Alright," I replied resigned. "Let me change and I'll meet you downstairs."

CHAPTER 6

As I was getting dressed, the odd sound of voices drifted through the open window, mingling with the sharp buzz of a saw. I crossed the hallway and peeked out of the spare bedroom window. There, on the front lawn, stood a small group of construction workers, clad in worn jeans and yellow hard hats.

A few weeks earlier, Beatrix, Gina's older-than-dirt neighbor, had driven her car straight into the house. The study, once used as Gina's home office, lay in ruins with a gaping hole carved into the front of the house. Today marked the first day the crew had arrived to fix the damage.

Gina and I made our way outside, stepping into the warm embrace of the sun. We waved to the crew as we strolled past. After climbing into Gina's vintage banana yellow mustang, she shifted into reverse. She had just started backing up when she slammed on the brakes, causing me to jerk against the seatbelt, nearly sending my head into the dashboard.

"What?" I stated.

"Someone was stupid enough to step behind the car while I was backing up. They're still standing there."

"What kind of idiot does that?"

Gina adjusted her rearview mirror, and a groan escaped her lips. "It's Lucinda."

That answered my question. "Can you back over her and pretend you didn't see her?"

"Good thought, but she already moved. She's heading straight for Jacob, looking like she's on a mission."

I looked out my window, catching sight of Lucinda as she engaged in an animated conversation with the construction foreman. Her voice was raised, and her arms were flailing dramatically, as if she was an air traffic controller.

"This can't be good," Gina said as we stepped out of the car.

Lucinda was wearing a skin-tight jumper with half her amplified double Ds hanging out of the top. Her collagen-injected lips twisted into a frown, and she wore enough makeup to rival a Kardashian. As soon as Gina approached, Lucinda launched into her tirade with barely a pause.

"All construction at this site must cease immediately until proper approval is obtained," Lucinda declared.

Gina, her hands resting firmly on her hips, met Lucinda's gaze with defiance. "I've already checked with the city. I don't need a permit to repair a damaged part of the house," she countered.

"True, but you didn't get permission from the historic society," Lucinda retorted, her eyes casting a judgmental glance over the project. "Every home within the city limits has guidelines that must be followed to preserve its historic integrity."

"I'm not making any changes," Gina insisted. "Jacob and his crew are simply restoring it to its original state after the accident." Jacob, who was standing beside her, nodded in agreement.

"Doesn't matter," Lucinda replied disdainfully, as she flicked an imaginary piece of lint from her shoulder. "I'm quite sure you didn't receive approval to paint your house this ghastly shade of yellow either."

Gina bristled at the remark, her hands on her hips tightening in response. "Your opinion really doesn't matter to me."

"It should," Lucinda shot back, narrowing her eyes, her lips turning up in a smug smile. "Not only am I the mayor's wife, but I also sit on the historic society board." With a flourish, she extracted a folded sheet of paper from her designer purse and handed it to Jacob. "It's my responsibility to ensure that the rules are upheld."

Jacob unfolded the document and scanned it. "It's a cease construction letter. We'll need to submit the construction plans to the historic committee for review at their next meeting."

Lucinda's lips curled into a self-satisfied smile. "We'll also be discussing changing this distasteful color of your house."

"When's the next meeting?" I asked.

"Three weeks from today," Jacob replied.

Gina took a step towards Lucinda, but I grabbed her arm, stopping her before she did anything that would land her in jail.

"Have a nice day," Lucinda remarked with a smile, her voice dripping with disdain as she pivoted on her three-inch heels and walked away.

"If she was any more of a bitch, she'd have puppies," Jacob muttered as he watched her saunter away.

"Now what?" Gina asked, frustration evident in her tone.

Jacob shrugged. "We're on hold. Unfortunately, the witch was right. Nothing else I can do until the historical society grants us permission." He let out a sharp whistle before yelling. "Alright, fellas, let's pack it up."

Gina's face flushed red with rage. "I'm going to get her."

"Let's not worry about her right now," I urged. "We have more pressing matters at hand."

* * * *

The town was alive with the peak tourist season, bustling with visitors eager to explore its historic charm. As we paused at a stoplight, I gazed around and took in the familiar streets adorned with vibrant colors. Baskets overflowed with flowers which dangled from vintage lamp posts, their scents mingling in the warm summer air. Bunting in the colors of red, white, and blue fluttered from the hotel windows, lending a patriotic feel to the scene. The street-front shops were inviting with their doors flung wide open, beckoning tourists to come in and peruse the treasures displayed on the sidewalks and inside.

We parked behind the building that housed Gina's private investigation business and set off on foot toward the hardware store, having to maneuver several blocks through the crowd. As we approached the corner of the parking lot, I noticed a small group of people gathered, their voices low and murmuring, their eyes drifting to the very spot where Sean had lain the night before. Word of the shooting must have gotten out already.

Out of curiosity, I walked over to see what was there, but all I saw was a patch of wet asphalt. The firetruck must have washed down the parking lot early this morning after police cleared the scene. I couldn't help but shake my head at the tendency of people to seek out gossip in the midst of tragedy.

I turned my attention back to the hardware store. Inside, a man stood behind the counter, clad in a forest-green shirt with the store's name sewn on one side of his chest and the name Luke on the other side. He was tall, over six feet, with a lanky build reminiscent of a basketball player. His dark brown hair was thinning at the temples, and he greeted us with a warm, friendly smile.

"What can I help you with?" he asked.

Gina stepped forward, handing him a business card. "We'd like to ask you a few questions."

"Private investigator," he noted, his eyebrows arching slightly in recognition.

Gina pressed on, "We wanted to ask you about last night."

For the briefest second, his smile wavered, a flicker of uncertainty crossing his face, but it was just long enough for me to catch it. "I don't know anything about that. The store closed at five last night."

"That seems early for tourist season," Gina remarked.

"Hardware stores aren't exactly a hotspot for tourists. We cater more to the locals," he replied.

"Was anyone else here when you closed the store last night?" I asked.

He nodded. "My brother Liam," he said, gesturing towards a figure coming around the counter. Liam matched his brother's height but sported striking gray eyes that set him apart. He wore a navy-blue ball cap with a picture of a cannon on it.

"I'm Sydney," I introduced myself. "Do you have any surveillance cameras on the property?"

Luke pointed towards the entrance. "We have one inside the door but none outside."

"Never saw a reason to install any outside before," Liam added.

"Do you have the tape from yesterday?" Gina inquired.

"No, the police took it this morning," Luke said.

"What time do you open in the morning?" I asked.

"We usually open at six for contractors, "Liam explained. "But the police were still here and didn't let us open until nine today."

A woman's voice rang out from across the store, calling for assistance. Without hesitation, Liam turned to help her, leaving us momentarily alone with Luke.

"Did you see anything suspicious when you left last night?" Gina asked.

Luke shook his head. "The parking lot was empty when we left." The phone on the wall rang. "I have to get back to work. Sean's a nice guy. I hope the police catch the person who shot him," With that, he answered the ringing phone, his attention shifting abruptly.

Gina and I stepped back into the blistering heat of the outdoors, the sun's rays hitting us like a wall of fire. I scanned the parking lot and the surrounding stores, searching for any hint of surveillance cameras. My eyes roamed over the scene, but I spotted none. Even the traffic lights were without cameras.

"You would think that someone would have spotted something last night," I stated flatly.

"This area is outside the tourist zone, and no hotels are nearby. Locals tend to retire early. Now what?"

"I can't believe I'm actually going to say this, but let's pretend to be tourists for the day."

Gina's eyes sparkled with excitement as she clapped her hands. "Let's buy matching Gettysburg t-shirts and hop on one of those tourist buses."

"Are you trying to give me a migraine?" I shot back. "We're simply going to stroll around the shops and see if anyone looks out of place."

"You're no fun," Gina replied deflated.

"Fine, you can buy a shirt," I conceded. "But none for me."

We spent the remainder of the morning wandering the main streets of town. As we wandered through the throngs of tourists, we kept a keen eye out for anyone who seemed disinterested in the historical charm or appeared disjointed from their group. We stepped into nearly every shop downtown.

By early afternoon, I was hot, hungry, and ready to shoot the next person who bumped into me. We strolled down the street where Genesis's pet grooming business was located. A colorful billboard on the sidewalk made me chuckle: "Neuter your dog, and your weird relatives and friends."

As we drew nearer, the church bell rang out its familiar, sonorous chime, marking the hour. Suddenly, a high-pitched whine erupted from inside the shop, quickly followed by a chorus of howling dogs. The commotion was almost deafening. Genesis burst through the door and firmly shut it behind her, blocking out the unpleasant symphony within. As the bell's relentless clanging came to a halt, the noise diminished to low, pitiful whimpers.

"Every time that bell rings the dogs go crazy," Genesis said, shaking her head with a smile that masked her frustration.

"It must hurt their ears," Gina said.

Genesis nodded in agreement.

"We're heading to the diner for lunch," I said. "Would you like to join us?"

"I can't," Genesis replied. "I must get Bella trimmed before the bell chimes again. She's a St Bernard, and not only is she the loudest barker, she almost broke the leash when the chiming started."

We waved goodbye and headed to Rita's diner.

The diner was packed with a mixture of locals and tourists. Every booth was occupied, and only a few tables remained which were rapidly dwindling in numbers. After we chose a table, we sat down and quickly placed our order with the waitress.

"I don't think we accomplished anything this morning," I said.

"That's not true," Gina replied, placing her hot pink plastic shopping bags on the table next to her. "I got a new 'I love Gettysburg' shirt and the cutest cannon-shaped earrings."

"Not quite what I meant," I sighed. "We're never going to track down the terrorists this way. We need a new strategy."

"They may not even be here," she suggested. "Maybe they were just passing through on their way to one of the bigger cities. We are nestled right in the middle of New York, DC, and Philly after all."

"Maybe," I said. "I'm just not sure." I conceded, but doubt lingered in my mind. I had a tendency to overthink things and fixate on the worst possible scenarios. It was a skill that served me well in my line of work, but here, in this quaint small town, it felt unnecessary.

It wasn't long before Indiah rushed over with our food. "This place is absolutely crazy today," she said as she placed our plates down in front of us. "I'm glad Mom hired some college students to help for the summer."

As she spoke, I followed her gaze to the entrance and spotted a group of men standing there. They were the construction crew that had been working at our house earlier that morning.

"You can have these two tables here," Indiah yelled to them.

They came over and pushed the two empty tables beside us together, and the eight of them picked their seats. Jacob nodded to us as he sat down.

"It still irks me that Lucinda stopped the construction on my house," Gina said.

"Well, there's nothing you can do about it now."

"Oh, I've got a plan," Gina replied, chomping down on a pickle.

I thought it best not to ask. As I sank my teeth into my chicken salad sandwich, savoring the mix of flavors, I spotted Troopers Rhode and Grant striding through the door. The busy diner continued to buzz around them, but they seemed to cut through the noise as they headed toward an open table in the corner. However, when Rhode spotted me, a frown settled on his lips, and he abruptly altered his course and started striding towards me.

"Heads up," I warned.

Gina turned in her seat. "Are those the two state police yahoos?"

Before I could respond, they stood beside our table, the air suddenly thick with tension.

"Ms. Hayes," Rhode addressed me, completely ignoring Gina. "Why didn't you tell me that you were at the crime scene last night?"

"Got my answer," Gina mumbled, stuffing a potato chip into her mouth with an exaggerated crunch. Rhode shot her a brief glance before his attention snapped back to me.

"You didn't ask," I said nonchalantly, taking a sip of cold water.

His lips pursed in evident annoyance. "Why were you at MY crime scene?"

I met his stare, my resolve strengthening. "It wasn't your crime scene at the time. We were driving home from my parents house when we noticed the police car parked in the Faulkner lot. It seemed deserted, which struck us as odd, so we decided to check it out."

"You just happened to be driving by?" Grant challenged, skepticism etched on his face.

I held his gaze steadily. "You are welcome to call my mother and verify our whereabouts."

Of course, we had taken a detour from the direct route between my parents house and Gina's, but he didn't need to know that little detail. He fixated his gaze on me for a moment, probably hoping to catch a flinch, but that wouldn't happen. I had mastered the art of deception, trained to lie with the finesse of a seasoned conman. He eventually broke the tense silence, diverting his gaze and pulling a worn notebook from his pocket. With a practiced flip of the cover, he turned his attention to Gina.

"Are you the Gina who was with Ms. Hayes last night?" he inquired.

"The one and only," Gina replied confidently, a slight smirk dancing on her lips.

"Do you have anything to add?" Rhode asked, his pen poised over the page.

"I do," Gina responded, reaching into her oversized shopping bag. With a flourish, she extracted a hardcover book. "Do you have any idea how many buildings in this town are haunted by Civil War ghosts?" She lifted the book high to display the cover, her eyes sparkling with excitement. "I've lived here my entire life and had no idea. Just bought this today so I can learn the fascinating history of the hauntings."

Rhode scrutinized Gina as if wondering why her hair wasn't blonde. He redirected his gaze towards me. "I heard you're also the one who discovered the body in the trunk?"

I took a bite of my sandwich, deliberately avoiding his question, which caused a flicker of irritation to cross his face. Grant stepped up beside me, assertively invading my personal space, as if aiming to seize my attention with his presence. "How did you know the body was in the trunk?" he probed, his tone sharpening.

I calmly lowered my sandwich back onto my plate, my glare piercing as I met his gaze with steely resolve. "By investigating," I replied. "You might want to try it instead of standing here interrogating me. In case you missed the memo, that's how crimes are solved."

"Watch how you speak to us," he shot back.

With a nod toward Rhode, he turned to make his exit. As they began to walk away, something caught my eye. Indiah approached, her tray laden with an assortment of drinks. As she drew near, I stuck my foot out, ready to disrupt her stride.

She stumbled, her foot snagging on mine, sending her sprawling off balance. A sharp gasp escaped her lips as she pitched forward, catching the attention of both troopers, causing them to turn around.

The metal tray flew off her hand, and the contents of the glasses and pitcher of water sprayed out all over the troopers, drenching their uniforms. They stood frozen, mouths agape, as droplets cascaded down them, the silence of the diner amplifying the clang of the tray tumbling to the floor and the shattering glass ringing out.

Indiah's hand flew to her mouth, eyes wide with horror. "I'm so sorry. My foot bumped into a chair leg, and I lost my balance," she stammered.

Before the troopers could muster a response, the door behind the counter burst open, and Rita, the owner of the diner, emerged with purposeful strides. She halted beside our table, taking in the chaotic scene of broken glass and the thoroughly drenched officers. "Please send your dry-cleaning bill to me," she remarked calmly. "And your next meal is on the house."

Rhode shot a scowl at Indiah, while Grant merely nodded, a trickle of dark liquid dripping from his ear. The entire restaurant remained as quiet as a church congregation until the troopers left. As soon as they disappeared, the murmur of conversations erupted once more.

Hands on her hips, Indiah shot me a puzzled look. "Why'd you trip me?"

I shrugged. "They made me mad."

Rita clicked her tongue disapprovingly, her eyes narrowing in playful annoyance. "You two still causing trouble," she said as she turned to walk away. "Still remember the time when Gina caught that cat on fire."

My eyebrow shot up in surprise, and I glanced at Gina, whose cheeks flushed slightly.

"Don't want to talk about it," she said.

"Let me help you clean up," I said, getting up to help Indiah.

Once we finished, I made my way to the cash register, the smell of coffee lingering in the air around me. I handed Indiah a stack of cash, enough cash to cover our meals, the dry-cleaning bill, and a meal for the troopers.

Out of the corner of my eye, I noticed a man seated at the counter, absorbed in the pages of the newspaper. The front page was prominently displayed, showcasing a vivid photograph of the Vice President waving cheerfully as he boarded a plane.

Indiah followed my gaze. "It's going to be a big event with him in town," she remarked. "They're expecting the tourist numbers to double, and I even heard the hotels are booked solid all the way to York."

A sudden realization struck me. "That's it," I exclaimed.

"What's it?" Indiah questions.

"Nothing, I've got to go." Without another word, I rushed toward the door, waving at Gina, who remained seated at the table.

As soon as we stepped outside, I turned to face Gina.

"I know, what's going on. The terrorists are here because of the Vice President."

CHAPTER 7

"You think they are going to try to assassinate the Vice President?" Gina asked, her voice low amidst the crowds of tourists.

I nodded. "Can you think of a better accomplishment than to take out a country's second in command? That would make headlines all over the world."

"I think you're on to something."

I started to pace on the sidewalk, which was hard with the tourists bustling around. "We need to dig deeper into his visit."

"We should ask Dad," Gina suggested. "He knows more about what's going on than anyone else, and even if he doesn't know something, he knows someone who does."

"Then let's go talk to him," I said, feeling a rush of urgency.

We returned to the office building, skirting around clusters of tourists taking pictures in front of historic structures. We spotted Krista coming through the glass doors as we approached the building.

"What are you doing here?" I asked, surprised to see her outside the hospital.

"Sean's parents are with him now," she replied, brushing a few strands of hair from her face. "I stopped to check on my cases, but Walter shooed me out. He told me not to return all week."

Gina's brow creased in worry. "You should be home resting."

With a dismissive wave, Krista shrugged off the concern. "I'm much too tired to sleep. I've already had four cups of coffee this morning."

"I thought you were a one-cup-a-day person," I asked as we stood in front of the building in the late afternoon sun. The rays beat down on my head, making me wish I had worn a hat today. I had only been in town a few months and was already becoming accustomed to the northern temperatures. If I stayed here too long, I would sizzle like bacon when I returned to the Middle East for an assignment.

"Too tired for just one cup this morning," Krista said before her eyes lit up, and her excitement bubbled out as if she had just spotted a movie star. "Not to change the subject, but you're never going to guess who I was just talking to."

Before either Gina or I could respond, the front door of the building swung open and out strolled Chase Mathis. His hair glimmered golden under the sunlight, and his bleached white teeth were almost blinding as he flashed us a radiant smile. Gina and Krista both let out a sigh as he strutted over to us.

"Sydney, I was just inquiring about your whereabouts with your sister, and here you are, just like magic," he said, extending his hand towards me. I kept my hands tucked firmly in the back pockets of my shorts. "How fortunate to run into you."

That was not quite my thought on the subject, but I managed to smile politely.

He flashed me a Hollywood smile, prompting Krista to giggle. "I was hoping you would join me for dinner tonight."

Gina gasped audibly, and I could almost hear Krista holding her breath in anticipation.

"You may have heard that my brother-in-law is in the hospital. I'll be spending my evening there to support Krista," I replied.

His smile didn't falter. It was as if he was oblivious to my reluctance. "I'm sure your sister will be willing to spare you long enough to enjoy a meal." He turned his striking smile to Krista.

She nodded enthusiastically like a bobblehead. I was convinced she was still holding her breath and sure she would start turning blue at any moment.

"Good," Chase said, returning his attention to me. "Then I insist you have dinner with me." Not one bead of sweat was on his brow, even though the summer heat made it feel like we were standing in Death Valley. He looked perfectly poised and confident.

What was I going to do? I didn't want to have dinner with Chase. Since he blocked my path to the law office building, I couldn't run into the building and lock myself in Gina's office. If I turned and walked down the sidewalk, I was certain he would follow like a shadow. I felt trapped as if I were in a room with a ticking bomb with no window or door for escape.

I spotted Blake striding across the sidewalk from the police station next door. He was headed towards his truck, which was parked at the curb. My window of escape opened just a crack.

"I'm sorry, I almost forgot that I already have dinner plans," I said as I hightailed it towards the rusted old truck parked at the curb. I yanked on the door handle, which creaked in protest, and plopped down on the seat next to a surprised Blake.

"What are you doing?" he asked.

"Just drive," I replied as I slammed the door shut.

Blake leaned forward and spotted Chase, who stood frozen in place, his expression one of surprise. Blake gave him a wave before turning the key in the ignition. As we pulled away from the curb, I glanced out the window. Krista's mouth was gaped open while Gina flashed a triumphant two thumbs up. Meanwhile, Chase pouted like a child. Since when did a grown man sulk? Clearly, he was too accustomed to getting his own way.

I exhaled as I settled into the cracked seat.

"So let me get this straight," Blake said, his voice tinged with disbelief. "You would rather hop into a vehicle with me and drive off to who knows where than spend time with Chase Mathis?"

"Don't flatter yourself," I shot back. "At this moment, I consider you the lesser of the two evils."

"Do you know you are hell on a man's ego?"

I shrugged. "Boosting your ego isn't my job."

"I've noticed," he said, tapping his thumb against the steering wheel. "You puzzle me. Most women in this town would be thrilled to have Chase's attention."

"Then they can have him. I'm not interested in dating."

He turned and gave me a look of disbelief.

"Believe what you like. I'm only here until my injuries heal, and then I'll return to my base in Italy."

"Maybe if you spent less time running around town playing Nancy Drew," he said teasingly. "You'd heal faster."

I held up a hand. "I'm not having this discussion with you."

He sighed. "You and everyone else. The state troopers have taken over Sean's office and refuse to discuss anything they uncover regarding the case."

I could practically feel his frustration radiating off him. I understood what it was like to have a fallen comrade. You wanted nothing more than to avenge the person. I felt sympathy for Blake, if only a little.

"If it makes you feel any better," I began. "Gina and I have been working on it all day, and honestly we haven't come up with any clear suspects." Which was true since we currently had no leads to follow.

Blake raised an eyebrow. "Would you tell me if you did?" Blake asked as he pulled his truck to a stop in front of Gina's house.

I considered his question for a moment before looking him in the eyes. "Probably not," I confessed, opening the door.

He chuckled softly. "At least you're honest," he replied and as I exited the vehicle he said, "and a very perplexing woman."

* * * *

After returning to the house, I raided the fridge for two cold beers. I placed one on the table between the two rocking chairs on the front porch for Gina. I unscrewed the top of the second to enjoy the refreshing cold brew while waiting for her.

I didn't have to wait long before Gina returned to the house. She climbed the stairs and stopped in front of me, shaking her head slowly, a mixture of frustration and amusement in her expression.

"You know why," I simply replied before finishing my beer with a final swig. I tossed it across the porch into the trash can in the corner, where it clanked against the other glass bottles within.

"It's been long enough," she said, taking a seat in one of the rocking chairs. "Besides, I'd sacrifice my left pinky toe to gain Chase's attention. Do you know he took over his family's business? Not only is he gorgeous, but he's also rich." She took a long swallow of the beer I had set out for her.

"Aren't you a little old for him?" I asked.

"I'm only seven years older than you."

"Still, that seems like a big age gap for dating. Would that make you a cougar?" I teased.

She gave me the finger.

"Let's go talk to Pap and see what he knows about the Vice President's visit. After that, we'll swing into the hospital. Maybe Sean will be out of his coma and able to tell us what happened last night."

"God willing," Gina said.

As I stood and reached for the screen door handle, I paused. "Do you realize," I said, a grin spreading across my face. "If you end up marrying Chase and having kids, you'll be an old lady walking with a cane by the time they finish college."

I chuckled as I ducked to avoid the bottle of beer Gina hurled at me. It sailed past my head, landing with a thud in the bush next to the porch.

* * * *

Pap was outside the barn washing his new SUV as we turned into the driveway. My mom stood near him, her arms animatedly gesturing as she spoke. The way she talked with her hands gave the impression that she was of Italian descent instead of German Irish.

She greeted us with a warm smile, but the corners of her lips quickly turned into a frown as we approached. My mother was old school, believing that women should dress modestly. Dresses should not reveal anything inappropriate, like cleavage or shoulders.

Gina's hot pink shorts and low-cut white V-neck shirt clearly didn't fit this image. My grey tank top and cargo shorts wouldn't pass muster either. My threadbare military boots probably pushed her over the edge.

"Are you two here for dinner?" she asked with a strained smile.

"No, we are heading over to the hospital to see Sean. We'll grab dinner with Krista," I replied.

My mother's half-hearted smile quickly dissolved into a frown. "I hope you don't plan on going out to a restaurant dressed like that," she said, planting her hands on her hips. "In my day no woman would dress like that."

Just then, Pap dropped the hose he had been holding onto the ground. Fortunately or unfortunately, depending on how you looked at it, the nozzle handle hit the ground first. A jet of water sprayed out of it, catching my mom in the face right in the middle of her rant. I bit my cheek to stifle a laugh as her expression shifted from indignation to surprise.

"I'm so sorry, Anita," Pap said, casting me a sideways wink.

Mom sighed. "It was an accident. I'm going inside to dry off and change." She scrutinized Gina and me one last time before scowling and walking away.

"What can I do for you?" Pap asked as he removed a soapy sponge from a bucket and scrubbed the vehicle's hood.

"We wanted to find out what you know about the Vice President's arrival in a few days?" Gina asked.

"I'm surprised that the two of you want to attend," he replied as he wiped down the headlights with the sponge.

"We don't. We just want to know what you know about the upcoming event," I said.

"Same as everyone else who reads the paper," he said, tossing the sponge back into the bucket with a splash, sending several bubbles floating into the air.

"We're hoping for more details, like when he'll arrive," I said.

"Or his route through town, or maybe how many Secret Service agents will be attending," Gina added.

I cringed knowing Pap would see right through his line of questioning.

Pap paused, picked up the hose, and rinsed off the SUV. "Why?"

I knew he wouldn't share any information unless we came clean. "We think someone may try to assassinate him during his speech."

He let go of the handle, turned off the nozzle, and stared at me. "Tell me what you know."

I went into detail about the body in the trunk, the missing skin, and the questionable link to the terrorist organization.

"That's pretty thin," he said skeptically. "You have no proof the tattoo even existed, let alone that there's a terrorist in town."

I kicked a small stone across the dusty ground. "I know."

"And your gut?" he asked, his gaze piercing mine.

I looked up. "Says that's something's not right."

He nodded. "Then we need to look into this." He dropped the hose to the ground and began striding purposefully towards the barn. I glanced at Gina, who shrugged, so we followed him inside. The air in the barn was heavy with the scent of hay and motor oil. He walked past the bay housing a pristine '69 Camaro and reached up to a dusty shelf behind it.

"The boys in DC are never going to believe you without solid proof," he said as he shifted around boxes and paint cans. My grandfather had served in the military long enough to know how often a mission was completed or a life saved because a soldier followed their instincts.

He pulled down a dusty old box, its lid open. Peering into the box, I noticed seven or eight cylindrical cardboard containers, each capped with white plastic ends, the kind of tubes typically used to store a poster. He carried the box over to the wooden table near the front wall. He dropped the box on the dirt floor, causing small clouds of dust to erupt around us.

He removed the brown tubes one by one and squinted at the faded labels, trying to read what was written on the side.

"Ha," he exclaimed as he read the inscription on the next-to-last cylinder. "This is it."

With a sweeping motion, he cleared the clutter of tools and miscellaneous items from the surface of the table, pushing them to the side. He then popped the cap off the tube and removed a rolled-up poster, its edges yellowing and frail. As he spread it across the table, I realized it wasn't a poster but a detailed map.

Pap flicked the switch on the wall, causing the fluorescent light overhead to buzz and blink twice before it finally turned on, illuminating the space with its harsh glow.

"You should replace that old light with one of the newer, brighter LED lights," Gina suggested.

As I inspected the map, I realized it was a detailed map of the town's center square.

"Why do you have a map of town?" I asked.

"Because there was no internet in my time," Pap replied. He traced his finger along the crinkled paper, landing it next to the Lincoln statue. "Here's where they're building the platform for the speech."

"So, what surrounding buildings do we have?" I asked, noticing the four largest buildings on the corners.

"These four are restaurants, and those two over there are stores," he explained, pointing at the designated buildings. "This," he said, directing my gaze to the imposing structure at one corner of the square, "is the bank. It will be closed that day, and on the other corner of the square is the hotel."

"What's on the upper levels of the restaurants and stores?" I asked, noticing each building was at least three stories tall.

"Mostly offices to the business beneath or office space they rent out," Pap replied.

"The speech isn't until evening, so most of the offices should be closed by then," Gina chimed in.

Pap rolled up the map, placed it back in the tube, and handed it to me. "Take this with you in case you need it."

"What are you girls up to?" came my dad's voice from the doorway.

"Pap will fill you in," Gina said. "We're heading out."

"You may want to pick up your pace. Your mother was putting her shoes on as I was leaving the house."

Gina gave her dad a quick peck on the cheek before we dashed toward the car. We were already backing out when my mom emerged from the house.

"That was close," Gina remarked, breathing a sigh of relief.

We were halfway to the hospital when my phone rang. I pulled it out of my pocket and glanced at the caller ID before answering.

"Hey," I answered Dominic.

"The license plate was a dud," he said. "It was a rental car paid for in cash, and the name on the receipt was Wolfgang Mozart. Really. Who doesn't recognize that as a fake name belonging to a famous composer?" he huffed with exasperation.

I couldn't help but smile. "Not everyone shares your deep love of music, you know."

"What's next on the agenda?" he asked with a hint of excitement. He obviously enjoyed the challenge of assisting us with this investigation.

I paused for a moment, letting the gears in my mind turn, then snapped my finger as an idea hit me. "The hotel. We need to know who's staying there."

"That would be an ideal location for an assassin to lay low," Gina said. "But hotels guard their guest lists."

"So, you want me to hack their system and pull the names of the current guests?" Dominic asked.

"Exactly," I confirmed.

"What kind of name should I be searching for? Something foreign?"

"No," I said. "Look for the most generic names you can think of, like John Smith or James Jones."

"Got it, the less memorable the better. Because they wouldn't use their real names," he said confidently. "It shouldn't be long. I'll have the list before morning." He ended the call with a click.

I stared out the window, wondering if we were on a wild goose chase.

"Don't stress," Gina assured me. "If there's nefarious business happening, we'll uncover it."

Yet, that was precisely what gnawed at me; the fear of what we might find.

CHPATER 8

As we entered the front lobby of the hospital, I noticed that the same graying older lady from last night was sitting behind the desk. Not surprisingly, she sat slumped in her chair, reading the same well-worn book. Her focus seemed unwavering, glued to the book, even as we approached the desk.

"Visiting hours are over," she announced as she stuck out her tongue to lick her finger before using it to flip the page.

I cleared my throat, which prompted her eyes to dart up. When she spotted me, she shot out of her seat as if it were covered with fire ants. Unsmiling, I cocked an eyebrow at her.

"Time for my break," she muttered hurriedly, nearly sprinting down the opposite hallway.

"I think she's scared of you," Gina remarked, a smirk playing on her lips.

I simply shrugged.

Krista was sitting in a chair next to Sean's bed. He lay there with his eyes shut, utterly still.

"Any updates on his condition?" I asked, standing beside the bed.

"The doctors said the swelling in his brain has decreased significantly. Tonight is the last time they're going to give him sedatives, and the doctor is expecting him to be awake by morning," Krista replied, her eyes sparkling with hope.

"That's fantastic news," Gina exclaimed.

Krista stood and stretched her tired muscles. "So what's happening with you?" she asked, her gaze locking onto mine.

"We have no leads on the case," I replied.

"That's not what I was talking about. I meant personally."

"Nothing."

"Bull. Chase asked you out, but you turned him down, then went and jumped in a vehicle with Blake."

"So," I replied, feeling the atmosphere in the room change to one of interrogation.

"Are you interested in Blake?" Krista asked.

"I wish," Gina said. "That man is so hot you could fry an egg on him." We both glanced at her. "What, I'm hungry."

"You're not interested in the two most eligible bachelors in town," Krista said, looking thoughtful. "Why?"

"I'm not here forever, remember," I responded, trying to deflect the question.

"That's not it," Krista said, crossing her arms over her chest. "There's something else. I can feel it."

Damn twin connection. A simmering tension enveloped the room as bubbling emotions churned inside me. A knot of unease tightened in my chest as thoughts of bolting out of the room conjured in my brain. Gina must have read my thoughts as she moved to stand in front of the exit.

"No more secrets," Krista reminded me.

"It's time," Gina said, her voice cutting through the stillness in the room.

"Fine," I replied, throwing my arms in the air. A sense of guilt gnawed at me, a constant reminder of the secrets I had kept from Krista for far too long. I had never enjoyed speaking about the past, and now it weighed on me. I walked past Krista to gaze out the window at the sky, painted in shades of purple and pink, as the sun set.

"I had a boyfriend..." I hesitated, the words caught in my throat like stones. "His name was Jason."

I turned towards Krista, who had her head tilted, curiosity shining in her eyes. "How long did you date?"

"Almost two years."

She arched an eyebrow but didn't respond.

"You have to understand," I continued. "Two years in army life isn't the same as civilian life. Most of the time, I was away or on a mission, or if I was home, he was gone."

The room was quiet for a moment as Krista sat back down in her chair.

"Why did the two of you break up?" she finally asked.

Gina turned her focus to the painting on the wall, her expression intent as though it held all the answers. Here was the question I knew was coming but dreaded. The one that used to haunt my thoughts and deprive me of sleep. I glanced back out the window but didn't focus on anything. I simply let the colors blur into a haze.

"We didn't," I finally said, wrestling with the weight of my secret. "Jason was a sniper. One day he left on a mission and never returned."

Tears, which one would expect to flow, did not come. I had already shed enough for Jason in the past. A flood of emotions surged within me, recalling the lighthearted anticipation I felt when I heard the knock at my door that fateful night. I had been expecting Jason, but instead, as I swung the door open, my Lieutenant stood there, his expression one of sorrow.

I heard the chair scrape across the floor as Krista sprang to her feet. She crossed the distance and gave me an unexpected hug from behind.

"How long ago did he die?" she asked, her voice laced with compassion.

"Three years ago," I said as I turned to face them. "I'm sorry I didn't tell you sooner."

A wave of anxiety washed over me. I was now aware of the possibility that Krista wouldn't find it in her heart to forgive me for once again hiding such a significant part of my life.

She smiled and gently squeezed my shoulder. "I understand. You were trying to keep your two worlds separate, weren't you?"

"Like a bigamous man with two families," Gina added.

I shot her a dirty look.

"That's a heavy weight to bear alone. Now that I know about your other life, I hope you'll let me into it."

"I'll never keep a secret from you again," I promised her.

"One more question." Krista raised her index finger. "Do you still love him?"

I shrugged, uncertainty swirling in my heart. "All I know is that I would never want someone I cared about to suffer with the same hurt if I someday never returned."

Krista nodded. "Fair enough. I won't try to fix you up with anyone again."

"Glad that's out in the open," Gina said, her tone lightening the mood. "Can we get something to eat now? I'm famished."

Krista glanced at Sean with uncertainty.

"You did say they sedated him, and he wouldn't be awake until morning," I reminded her.

"I guess it wouldn't hurt to leave for an hour or so," she said, a smile gracing her lips before she leaned in to plant a gentle kiss on his cheek.

As we walked out of the building towards the car, I noticed worry etched across Krista's brow.

"What are you worried about now?" Gina asked.

"Sean and I tell each other everything," she replied. "How am I supposed to keep all this from him?"

I thought about it for a moment. "When you think he's ready, go ahead and tell him." I felt a weight beginning to lift from my shoulders. Maybe I should have confided in my family sooner. Perhaps I would have visited home more often if I hadn't felt that heavy cloud of deceit hanging over my head.

"Don't give away all my secrets, though," I added, giving her a wink.

* * * *

Gina made a detour at the grocery store on our way to dinner. When I asked what she was picking up, her response was, "It's going to rain tonight." I didn't bother to probe the significance of her statement. Honestly, I was afraid to ask, so Krista and I chose to remain in the car while she dashed inside.

A short while later, we pulled up to a restaurant with a vibrant red tile roof and a bamboo archway framing the entrance.

"This is a hibachi grill," Gina said as we exited the car. "I thought we could use a little entertainment tonight."

I smiled, recalling my last visit to a place like this. "I haven't been to one of these in years."

"They have hibachi restaurants in Rome?" Krista asked.

"Actually, it was in Morocco."

"Did you enjoy it?" Krista asked as she held the door open for me to enter.

"It was cut short when the guy I was with was shot in the head." I walked past her, leaving her momentarily frozen, her eyes wide in shock as she covered her mouth with her hand.

"I'm so sorry," she stammered.

"No loss," I replied nonchalantly. "I was on a mission, and he was an illegal wildlife smuggler. I was just about to bust him for trafficking Barbary Macaque monkeys into America when someone shot him first."

Krista stared at me for a moment, her expression a mix of disbelief and intrigue, as if she were seeing the true me for the first time. "Your life is so weird. Remind me to never ask you about it again," she said. "Ever," she added for emphasis, shaking her head.

The hostess escorted us through the lively dining room to the central area, where one of the large tables encircled a flat grill. Five guests were already seated at the table, smiling at us as we approached. We slid into our seats at the end of the table, with Gina choosing the corner spot.

"Good," a man at the table boomed. "The table's finally full, now we can eat."

The woman beside him, who I assumed was his wife, nudged him with her elbow. "Don't mind, Larry. We were the first to be seated, so we've been waiting a while."

A Japanese chef, dressed in a crisp button-up white shirt and black pants, approached our table, pulling his cart of supplies behind him. He parked his cart next to Gina and placed his hands together in front of himself, bowing and pronouncing, "Konnichiwa."

As he leaned over his cart, he revealed two large steel spatulas, with wooden handles. With precision, he began to work, expertly scooping bowls of fluffy rice, vibrant vegetables, and pieces of chicken onto the sizzling grill. The food began to hiss and crackle, releasing a rich array of aromas that danced through the air, tantalizing my taste buds.

He captivated us with his skills, juggling the utensils as he chopped up the food in front of him. He then pushed the freshly prepared food to the side of the grill and reached for an onion sitting on the cart beside him. Carefully, he sliced the onion into thin circles and expertly stacked them on top of one another, forming a round pyramid.

Gina clapped enthusiastically. "The flaming onion is my favorite part," she exclaimed.

"Anything involving fire is always your favorite part," I teased.

The chef retrieved a plastic squirt bottle from the cart. He carefully squirted the contents into the small hole at the top of the onion tower.

He pulled a lighter from his pocket and flicked it open, producing a small flame. He held it above the tower, and instantly, flames of blue and yellow erupted from the center of the onion. I could feel the warmth of the fire on my face.

"What accelerant do you think they use to start the fire?" Gina asked, her eyes sparkling with curiosity.

"Maybe cooking oil," Krista suggested.

I remained silent as my cooking skills were limited to meals that came in boxes with microwave instructions.

As the flames in the onion began to dwindle, the chef started to portion out the food and deposited it on the waiting plates. Leaning over my plate, I inhaled deeply, savoring the mouth-watering aroma that wafted up. My gaze shifted as I noticed Gina leaning over the side of her chair, her expression alight with mischief.

"What are you doing?" I asked.

"Just looking," she replied as she straightened back up, holding a bottle in her hand. The glass bottle was crystal clear, filled with a transparent liquid, and devoid of any labels or markings.

"What do you think is in it?" she asked, lifting the open-topped bottle to her nose.

"Put that back before you cause trouble," I warned.

"I'm just smelling it," she insisted, taking a few tentative sniffs. "Smells grainy like bread," she took a deeper whiff. "Maybe a hint of lemon."

"You are not stable," I said.

The chef turned at my words, his eyes narrowing as he noticed the bottle in Gina's hand. "No, No." he shouted in his fractured English, urgency lacing his voice. "100 proof!"

He snatched the bottle from Gina, but his grip faltered. The bottle slipped from his fingers, crashing down onto the grill with a resounding shatter. Glass shards scattered like confetti while the potent liquid gushed out, running across the hot surface. Once the fiery remnants of the onion met the high-proof spirit, the entire grill ignited, erupting in a blaze that illuminated the room like a redneck bonfire.

Pandemonium ensued as diners sprang from their seats, eyes wide with shock. Flames leaped toward the ceiling. Out of the corner of my eye, I caught sight of the chef's shirt sleeve engulfed in fire. He flailed his arm desperately, resembling a frantic chicken.

"I'm on fire!" he hollered as he ran into the kitchen, leaving the chaos behind him.

The patrons began a hasty retreat towards the exit. Gina pointed urgently toward her purse, which was perilously close to the growing inferno. The purple leather was bubbling ominously, threatening to catch fire at any moment.

"How many explosives do you have in there?" I asked.

Gina's eyes darted toward the ceiling as her head swayed from side to side as if she was actually tallying an invisible number. I muttered a curse under my breath as I snatched a long spatula from an abandoned grill nearby. I used it to lift the handle of the purse and drag it away from the flames, which seemed to be growing larger with each passing second.

I moved to a nearby table to deposit the scorched purse, but just as I reached it, the bottom tore open. The contents spilled out onto the table, causing us all to recoil, wincing at the potential disaster. When a moment passed without an explosion, we cautiously looked back.

On the table sat ordinary items, such as a wallet and a tube of lipstick, but among these were two guns, a hunting knife, a pocketknife, and two sticks of dynamite, whose fuses, fortunately, were intact. Alongside it was a glass vial containing a mysterious green liquid adorned with a crudely drawn skull in black marker.

"Call of Duty has seriously warped your perspective on the number of weapons you need to carry," I said.

"I really need to make some new friends," Krista added.

The fire was still going strong and was now spreading across the wooden table. Thick smoke billowed upwards, swirling around the room. Little licks of flame were spurting out as if the fire itself was spitting. The small balls of flame were falling onto the carpet, which instantly ignited.

"Who puts carpet in a restaurant these days?" Gina asked, her eyes wide in disbelief.

"That's your main concern with this situation?" I shot back, aggravated. "The carpet?"

"Why hasn't the sprinkler gone off?" Krista asked, pointing at the silver sprinkler head protruding from the ceiling above the raging inferno.

As my eyes started to burn from the smoke, I seized a drinking glass from the table behind me and hurled it at the sprinkler. It hit its mark perfectly, which caused a torrent of water to gush forth and douse the flames on the table.

Suddenly, an ear-piercing siren filled the room. The activation of the sprinkler had not only triggered the alarm but also awakened adjacent sprinklers, including the one above our heads.

"Grab your stuff and let's go," I yelled at Gina, straining to be heard over the sound of the screaming alarm as water rained down on us.

Gina grabbed her shirt hem, and we loaded all her purse items into the front of her clothes. Once everything was stowed away, she lifted the bottom of the shirt to her chest, creating a pouch, and we dashed towards the exit. My foot had just touched the pavement when the first firetruck screeched into the parking lot.

"A little late now, "Krista remarked, her fingers gripping her damp strawberry-blonde hair as she wrung out the excess water.

"Ooh, firemen," Gina said.

Krista and I exchanged amused glances and burst into laughter.

"What?" Gina said.

"Your mascara has smeared, making you look like a raccoon," Krista pointed out.

"And with you holding your shirt up like that," I chimed in, "your stomach is so pale it makes a sheet of paper look colorful."

Gina stuck her thumbnail behind her front teeth and flicked it out at us. She then proceeded over to her car to deposit her purse supplies.

"Does she know a curse gesture in every language?" Krista asked.

"Probably," I laughed, shaking my head.

Moments later, Gina returned, her face clear of makeup and the residual raccoon eyes. "Now, how do I look?" she asked.

"You need a bra with padding," said the woman standing next to us, who had been sitting at our table. "You look like you were in a wet t-shirt contest."

Her husband shot us a grin. "Not that anyone's complaining," he quipped, only to receive an elbow in the ribs from his wife hard enough to elicit an "umf".

Krista glanced at her gold watch. "Guess we should stop for some fast food on the way back to the hospital."

With a collective nod of agreement, Gina and I fell in step beside her, making our way back to the car.

* * * *

The hospital was enveloped in an unusual quiet when we returned, an eerie calm that contrasted with the hustle and bustle we had experienced during the day. Over half the lights in the corridor were turned off, creating a more nighttime atmosphere.

As we approached the room, a solitary figure in a white lab coat emerged from Sean's room. Their posture was slumped, eyes fixed on the ground, and without a single glance in our direction, they headed the opposite way down the hall.

"Was that a doctor?" Gina whispered.

"His doctor said he wouldn't be back until tomorrow?" Krista replied.

A chill ran down my spine, prickling the hairs at the back of my neck, a clear warning bell that was never a good sign.

CHAPTER 9

We rushed down the white-walled corridor, the only sound penetrating the silence was the crinkling of the fast-food bags. Upon entering the room, everything appeared normal. Sean lay peacefully sleeping in the bed while the array of machines around him hummed softly. I rolled my shoulder, attempting to ease the tension I had felt from the false alarm.

Just as I thought we were in the clear, Krista's voice cut through the air. "Why is the liquid in the IV a different color in this one area?"

I looked at the tubing, and sure enough, the fluid just below the pump was a milky tan, contrasting with the clear liquid in the rest of the line. We exchanged anxious looks as it hit us that someone had added something to Sean's IV.

"Turn it off!" I shouted as I dropped my food bag onto the foot of the bed.

Krista frantically began pressing buttons on the pump. Meanwhile, Gina rushed to the bedside, pressed the bright red button that called for the nurse.

"N-nothing's happening," Kirsta said, panic in her voice as the pump continued its slow task of pushing the discolored liquid closer toward Sean's arm.

Gina reached behind her and unplugged the machine, but nothing changed. It must have been equipped with a battery backup.

"Now what?" Krista said.

Without thinking twice, I grasped the IV line at the place it fed into Sean's arm, ripping it out with a swift motion just as a nurse in navy scrubs stepped into the room, her expression shifting from calm to alarm.

"What's going on in here?" she demanded, looking at Sean's arm, which was now seeping blood where the IV had been.

"Take care of this," I said, not waiting for her response as I pushed past her. I sprinted down the hallway in the direction the intruder had gone. Halfway down the corridor, I paused, swiftly extracting my nine-millimeter from the small of my back, ready to confront whatever awaited me.

I cautiously made my way down the dimly lit hall with my gun drawn, my focus honed on the slightest sound that might betray the intruder's position. The solitary fluorescent light overhead flickered unpredictably, emitting a soft buzz with each flicker. It created an eerie atmosphere, mimicking a scene from a horror movie.

Suddenly, the distinct sound of running water from a nearby sink broke the silence. The stick figure on the door indicated it was a bathroom. The water stopped, and after a few seconds, the receptionist emerged. She was drying her hands on a paper towel, oblivious to the turmoil unfolding around her. When she looked up and spotted me standing there with my gun in hand, she turned white as a ghost.

"What's at the end of this hall?" I asked.

Her mouth opened several times like a fish gasping for air, but no sound came out. Finally, she stammered, "Break room," before darting away down the hall in a panic.

As my gaze shifted from her retreating form, I caught movement out of the corner of my eye. A shadowy figure dressed in black darted from a room and slipped through a door at the end of the corridor.

I sprinted towards it and burst through the door into the stairwell. I grabbed onto the railing to keep myself from plummeting down the stairs. As soon as I steadied myself, I bolted down the stairs like a bullet.

I emerged into the night at the side of the building, my eyes scanning the darkness. There, I spotted the dark figure jumping into the passenger seat of a black truck, which sped off before the door had a chance to close fully. I took off after it but wasn't able to catch a glimpse of the full plate number before it turned onto the main road, disappearing from sight. Frustrated, I kicked a boulder at the entrance, which only caused me pain, adding to my irritation. I spun in circles on one foot for a moment, cursing before heading back towards the hospital.

I figured the door to the stairwell would be locked, but I tried the handle just in case the intruder had slipped in this way. As expected, it didn't budge. Muttering under my breath, I rounded the building and stepped back inside through the front door. The receptionist was nowhere in sight. She was probably experiencing a coronary and was lying behind the desk unconscious. I didn't have the energy to investigate her fate.

When I entered the room, Blake was standing at the foot of the bed with a half-eaten carton of French fries in his hand. My food bag now laid open on the bed.

"Do you mind?" I asked, snatching my bag from the bed.

"I left you the burger," Blake replied, popping another fry into his mouth.

Next to Krista stood a tall man in a white lab coat.

"Sydney, this is Doctor Shiver," Krista introduced. "We were just telling Blake and him what happened."

"After which you thought the best option was to chase after the perp," Blake chastised.

"Unfortunately, he got away," I replied. I relayed the description of the vehicle and the first three letters of the license plate that I was able to see before it sped off.

"Not much to go on, but I'll see what I can do," Blake said, tossing the empty fry container into the trash bin. His gaze then swept over me. "Is it raining outside?" he said, barely managing to keep a straight face.

"Ha, ha," I replied dryly. "You already know the answer, don't you?"

"Officer Kline was pulling into the parking lot of the restaurant as Gina's Mustang was pulling out. He couldn't wait to fill me in on what had happened."

I pursed my lips tightly as I circled around him, stopping to survey the puddle of liquid that had pooled on the floor under the IV tubing.

"What do you think was injected into that IV line?" I asked the doctor.

The doctor's brow furrowed in contemplation. "It's hard to say. Could have been anything."

"If you tested it, would you be able to identify the poison?" Krista asked.

He shook his head. "It didn't have to be a poison. Almost any liquid pushed directly into the bloodstream could prove fatal."

A small cry escaped Krista, and Gina wrapped her arms around her. The doctor continued.

"It could have been something as common as household ammonia or vinegar. Even coffee." His gaze shifted to Krista as if to gauge her reaction. "Like I said, anything could have grave effects. We can't test for everything."

I opened my mouth to respond, but the entrance of troopers Grant and Rhode cut me off. They surveyed the crowd.

"What's going on here?" Grant demanded.

Krista and Gina took turns recounting the dire event.

"Are you going to have an officer watch over Sean to protect him?" Krista asked.

Trooper Grant responded dismissively, "I don't see why."

"You're kidding, right?" I shot back. "Someone just tried to kill him. Most likely, the person who shot him in the first place is behind this."

"Exactly," Gina chimed in. "They probably don't want him to identify them when he wakes up."

Grant turned towards the doctor. "Doctor, can you say with certainty that someone was here and attempted to poison this patient?"

The doctor hesitated. "No, but-"

"There you go," Grant interrupted. "All I see is a puddle of liquid on the floor and three hysterical women who may or may not have witnessed something."

My hands clenched into fists, and I took a half step forward, ready to confront the troopers. Just then, I felt a firm grip on the back of my shirt holding me back.

Blake leaned down and whispered in my ear, "If anyone gets to punch him, it will be me."

At that moment, another officer entered.

"Officer Beck, what are you doing here?" Blake asked.

"Sorry, detective. We received a frantic call from a distraught employee about a crazy person with a gun wandering the hospital," Officer Beck replied.

Blake glanced at me, and I shrugged, feigning ignorance. "I can't say for certain if the intruder was armed or not." I said, fully aware that the receptionist had reported me as the 'crazy person.'

"Did you locate the individual?" Blake asked.

The officer shook his head.

Blake nodded. "Officer Beck, I'm reassigning you. You'll take up a post outside this room to secure the area and protect Sergeant Wallace."

Officer Beck's eyebrows shot up in surprise, but he nodded in compliance.

"No one except hospital staff or individuals currently in this room is allowed to enter without going through me first," Blake said.

Trooper Grant interjected, crossing his arms defiantly. "You can't do that. This isn't your investigation."

Blake met Grant's gaze, unflinching. "Protecting the life of one of my officers is of utmost importance and has nothing to do with your case. It won't hinder your investigation," he replied, his tone leaving no room for debate.

The troopers stormed out of the room, their heavy boots thudding against the floor. I'm sure they would have knocked Officer Beck over if he hadn't moved out of the way. Blake shook his head.

"Scumbags," Gina said, her voice laced with disdain. Everyone in the room nodded in agreement.

Officer Beck picked up one of the chairs and quietly exited the room.

"Everyone go home and get some rest, including you, Krista," Blake said. "Officer Beck will watch over Sean, and I'll have him call you if he wakes up."

Krista nodded, exhaustion etched in every muscle of her body.

"We'll give you a ride home," Gina said, and the three of us made our way out into the cool night air.

* * * *

As we dropped Krista off, jagged bolts of lightning pierced the sky and thunder rolled along the mountains. Gina was right, it was going to storm. We drove towards town, but at the last moment, she turned onto a road, two streets before her own.

"Where are we going?" I asked, my voice tinged with exhaustion. It had been a long day, and after spending the night sitting upright in a hospital chair, it barely counted as rest, let alone sleep. I felt like a zombie and wanted to crawl into bed and sleep for the next twelve hours.

"Quick stop on the way," she said, pulling the car to the curb several houses down from the corner, hiding behind a white SUV. She scanned the surroundings cautiously, but the streets were deserted, the only sound was the distant rumble of thunder.

"I know what you are up to," I said.

Gina raised an eyebrow and smiled. "Really?"

I peered behind us, confirming my suspicion. "Lucinda's house is two doors back."

"But you don't know what I've got planned." She lifted the plastic grocery bag from the backseat. "This is going to be brilliant."

Just then, a bolt of lightning pierced the sky.

"It's going to start raining any minute," I protested.

"And you're afraid to get wet?" she teased, looking over my still-damp hair and clothes.

She pulled the tab next to her seat, popping the trunk open with a small click before getting out of the car. For a moment, I sat there, calculating our chances of getting struck by lightning. After weighing my options, I deemed it a low risk and climbed out of the car. When I rounded the trunk, she extended her hand towards me.

"Hold this," she said, handing me a crowbar as casually as if she were offering me a cup of coffee instead of a tool meant for breaking and entering. She fished a hammer from her trunk before quietly closing the lid.

"Why do you have a hammer and crowbar in your trunk?" I couldn't stop myself from asking.

"Part of my emergency kit," she replied as though it was entirely natural for someone to carry such items in their vehicle. I couldn't help but picture what would happen if she ever got pulled over. With what she kept in her trunk, it would probably be a one-way ticket to jail.

We slipped into Lucinda's neighbor's backyard and stopped behind a large pine tree. Lucinda's back fence was in front of us. Handing me the grocery bag, Gina took the crowbar.

"You keep watch," she whispered. Kneeling down, she gripped the crowbar tightly. She began to pry at the base of one of the fence planks. The nail squeaked and groaned as it was forced from the wood. It cut through the stillness of the night, sounding as if it were coming from a loudspeaker.

"Keep it down," I urged, looking around the pine tree for any house lights.

"You are welcome to try if you think you can do better," she shot back. At last, the nail finally gave way with a sigh, allowing the bottom of the board to pop free. She pivoted the plank aside, creating a narrow opening at the bottom of the fence. She gestured for me to hand her the grocery bag.

From it, she retrieved a small plastic canister adorned with a red label. With a twist, she unscrewed the lid and, in one fluid motion, flung the contents into Lucinda's backyard.

As a crack of thunder roared, a faint aroma of steak wafted through the air.

"What was in the container?" I whispered.

"Beef bouillon cubes," Gina replied, her eyes scanning the darkness as she stood up. Without hesitation, she bolted across the yard, ducking behind an oak tree. I followed even though I knew the tree trunk was not big enough to conceal us both. As I pressed against the rough bark, Gina went to work on loosening another board.

"What do you hope will happen?" I asked.

"I hope the rain will soak the beef smell into the ground. Then maybe a neighborhood animal will come sniff around and scare Lucinda."

She hurled another container of beef cubes through the newly created gap in the fence. Suddenly, a bright light flickered on from the house whose backyard we were occupying.

"Someone's up," I whispered. I spotted a low-hanging branch to my left and jumped up to grab it. Using it as leverage, I hoisted myself up into the tree. I climbed up several more branches until I was sure I was high enough for the leaves to conceal me from view.

"Show off," Gina mumbled as she stood up, turning sideways and plastering herself up against the tree.

Moments later, the backyard was flooded with light. A man clad only in his boxers emerged cautiously onto the porch, scanning the yard.

"I don't see anything," he said to a woman who was peeking her head out from behind the sliding glass door.

"I heard something," she insisted.

"Probably a rabbit or something," he said, scratching his butt. "It's gone now." With a shrug, he reentered the house, pulling the door shut behind him.

Just moments after the floodlights went out, rain started to fall in a steady drizzle. I waited several minutes before climbing down out of the tree.

"Did you see that guy?" Gina asked, her voice tinged with amusement. "He had more hair on his back than a grizzly."

In that instant, it felt as if the gates of heaven had opened, unleashing a torrential downpour from the clouds above.

"Let's get out of here before we drown," I urged.

We darted behind the shelter of the trees and quickly made our way to the sidewalk. Once we reached the car, Gina slammed the door and hit the gas, sending us racing down the rain-soaked road.

CHAPTER 10

The next morning, I was dragged from my slumber by the resonant baritone toll of the church bell. I rolled over, burying my head beneath the pillow, silently cursing the clanging. The pillow offered some minor noise control, but it wasn't enough to drown out the sound completely. With a resigned sigh, I crawled out of bed.

I found Gina in the kitchen grumbling, "I hate that bell," as she dumped dark coffee grounds into the machine. Neither one of us felt like putting effort into making breakfast, so we resorted to rummaging through the pantry and pulling out a box of Pop-Tarts. As I took my first bite, the pastry crumbled apart in my mouth, taking on the unpleasant texture of sawdust.

"How old is that box?" I asked after taking a drink of coffee to wash the stale taste down.

"I don't know," she replied, picking up the box to examine it. "It was left here when I moved in."

"And you didn't take that as a hint to throw it out?" I raised an eyebrow, a mix of disbelief and amusement flickering across my face.

"It expired two years ago," she said as she tossed her pastry back into the box.

I seized the box and threw it in the trash. As I returned to the table, I noticed Gina leaning out the window, her eyes scanning the backyard.

"What are you looking at?"

"Nothing. That's the problem," she responded. "Where are my chickens?"

"Maybe they're in the coop," I said, peering out the window of the back door.

"Cagney didn't come for her breakfast," Gina declared, a note of worry creeping into her voice.

Now I wondered where they could be. Since moving into the house, the chickens had made it a daily ritual to hop up on the windowsill every morning expecting a piece of Gina's meal.

Gina jumped out of her chair and headed towards me. "If Oscar did something to those chickens," she said as she stormed out the back door with me following in her wake. I could feel her anger as she yanked the fence gate open, the old wood creaking in protest, as if the gate was going to come off its hinges.

Once we reached the driveway, I spotted Cagney standing at the edge of the neighbor's yard.

"There's Cagney," I said, pointing her out to Gina.

As we approached, the chicken seemed oblivious to our presence. Her gaze was fixed on the neighbor's house.

"Where's Lacey?" Gina asked the chicken.

Following Cagney's gaze, I spotted Lacey perched on the small overhang of the porch roof of the neighbor's house.

Just then, Oscar burst through the front door. "What are you doing in my yard?" he demanded.

It was hard to take his anger seriously given his choice of attire. He was dressed in a white, long-sleeved shirt with two buttons fastened at the collar that flowed down to his knees. It resembled a woman's nightgown. Beneath it, he wore white slippers that added to the ridiculousness of the scene. I couldn't help but picture him with a matching triangular night cap with the pom-pom ball on top, like a character from one of those old children's stories. I giggled at the sight.

"Is that what you're wearing today?" Gina teased.

"This is an authentic pajama shirt from the 1800s that men wore to bed," he remarked with pride.

"He takes his history seriously," I whispered to Gina.

"As you know, I play Major General Winfield Hancock in the reenactment," he stated smugly as if the role he played made him more important.

Cagney flapped her wings in protest, as if to remind him he wasn't as important as he thought. At least that's how I interpreted it.

"Get that foul off my property," he exclaimed, taking a step forward. Cagney let out a loud squawk. At the sound, Lacey squatted down and laid a smooth brown egg that rolled down the roof. As the egg picked up speed, it met Oscar's unsuspecting head at the exact moment he advanced down the stairs. On impact, the egg cracked open, showering him with its contents. The bright yellow yolk oozed down his forehead and trickled down the bridge of his nose.

Cagney happily hopped from one foot to the other excitedly. With a flap of her wings, Lacey launched herself from the roof, gracefully floating down before landing on Gina's shoulder, cooing softly as if to celebrate the mess she had caused.

I glanced at Gina and we both erupted with laughter.

"Stupid chickens," Oscar said as he took a step towards us, egg dripping off his nose.

The chickens took that as their sign to exit, and they quickly waddled back through the open gate to the back yard with their feathers rustling softly.

"You better wash that egg off before it stains your dress," Gina teased.

Oscar looked down at his shirt, frowning at the yellow spot that now marred his once clean attire.

"I'm reporting this assault to the police," he declared as he dashed back up the stairs. "You're buying me new pajamas."

"I'll look in the plus-sized women's section for you," Gina shot back.

A car horn honked as Dominic pulled his sleek Porsche into the driveway. With a reputation as a computer genius, Dominic had struck gold by selling an app to a major tech company, allowing him to retire early. Nowadays, he only used his hacking skills for sheer enjoyment.

As he swung open the car door, he reached across the seat and held up a bakery box.

"I brought muffins," he announced. "Did I miss any action this morning?" He cast a glance towards the neighbor's house. "And was he wearing a nightgown?"

"I'll fill you in later," I said, lifting the lid of the box, enjoying the sweet scent of the pastries. "I thought you loved to cook?" I added.

"With that bell waking me up this morning, I was just too tired to bother."

We headed up the front path, which was now covered with debris from the storm the previous night.

"Look at all these spinners from my maple tree," Gina groused.

"That storm last night was wicked," I said, settling into the rocking chair on the porch. "It was still raining at three o'clock this morning."

"I thought the maple tree seeds were called whirlybirds?" Dominic stated.

"Whatever," Gina replied as she retrieved her garden hose from the side of the porch. She was almost finished spraying off the front walk when a car rolled to a stop in front of the house, and Rhode and Grant exited.

"Great," I sighed.

"Friends of yours?" Dominic asked, popping the last morsel of his muffin into his mouth.

"Not quite."

The two men approached the walk, stopping short of the spray from the hose.

Rhode looked stern as he spoke, "We just came from the hardware store. We were informed that you were there yesterday asking questions about our investigation." He fixed Gina with a stern gaze. "Can you turn the hose off?"

"Certainly," she replied as she bent to twist off the faucet. But as she did, her arm swung back behind her, unintentionally launching a blast of water all over Rhode's polished shoes. He cursed and leaped back.

"Oops," Gina said with feigned innocence as she dropped the hose.

"Is that appropriate language to use while you're working?" Dominic asked Rhode.

Rhode ignored him. "Ms. Hayes why are you sticking your nose into our investigation?" he asked, annoyance lacing his tone as he shook his foot in a futile attempt to rid his shoe of the water.

"I was only making polite conversation while we were at the store," I replied.

"I'm not an idiot," he stated.

He had yet to prove that point to me.

"If we catch you meddling in our case again, we will have no alternative but to charge you with obstruction of justice and have you arrested." He merely nodded and turned away, his right shoe making slushing sounds with each step.

"Gonna have to keep a spare set of clothes in the trunk for as long as we're in this town." I heard Grant remark as they returned to their vehicle.

"Police officers don't seem to like you," Dominic said to me.

I shrugged.

"Let's get down to business," Gina said, coming on the porch and plopping down on the swing, the chains groaning under her weight. I handed her the muffin box. "What did you find out about the hotel guests?"

"No plain names but there was one interesting lead," Dominic replied. "A Daniel Craig is staying in room three eleven."

"Definitely stands out," Gina said before taking a bite of her blueberry muffin, crumbs tumbling down her shirt. "Who wouldn't want to be 007?"

"It's the only lead we have," I said.

"Have you thought of an air bed and breakfast?" Dominic asked.

"A what?"

Dominic rolled his eyes. "Please tell me you heard of it?"

I shook my head.

"It's a short-term house rental," he explained. "It is so the way to vacation now. Everyone's doing it. Don't they have them in Europe?"

"I was there for work, not vacationing," I replied.

"It's great," Dominic said with a grin. "You get a whole house to yourself. It would be a perfect way for a group of people to all stay in one place, away from prying eyes."

"Do you think they have some around here?" I asked.

"Most definitely," he replied. "A lot of times they're rented through local real estate agencies."

I glanced at Gina. "The only real estate agency in town is Adams County Reality across the hall from my office. We can check it out first thing this morning."

Dominic stood up, stretching slightly as he prepared to leave. "Well, I'm off. I'm heading out of town to my own B&B for a few days to avoid the crowds in town for the reenactment. Call me if you need anything."

With a final wave, he strode away, jumping into his car before driving off. The sound of the engine faded into the distance.

* * * *

About an hour later, we were pulling up in front of the office building where Gina worked. We lingered in the car, patiently waiting for the clock on the church steeple to finish its ninth chime, the sound echoing through the quiet street.

Inside the real estate office, the small lobby featured a striking picture window that faced the street, allowing natural light to spill in and illuminate the space. Comfortable chairs were neatly arranged along the window. In the center of the room stood an empty reception desk. Behind the desk were two offices, each separated by a narrow hallway. Behind the office on the left was a second office, and behind the office on the right was a conference room with a long table and eight chairs surrounding it. I knew this because all the walls were made of glass. Floor-to-ceiling glass surrounded each office, held together by silver metal beams.

To the left, the second office was occupied by a red-headed woman, engaged in a phone conversation. Her bright hair framed her face, and as she noticed us, she paused to hold up one finger, signaling for us to wait just a moment. To the right, the front office contained a man in his late twenties, his attention fixed on the glow of the computer screen, brows furrowed in concentration.

"If my office were made of glass, it would give me hives," Gina said. "I would feel like I was trapped in a reptile aquarium with someone watching my every move."

"Afraid they'd catch you playing with matches," I teased as I stepped closer to the wall and gently tapped on the glass to the first office.

The man's head jerked up at the sound and he gave me a friendly smile. He rose from his desk and exited the human terrarium. He was casually dressed in a pair of jeans and a pale green shirt.

"Sorry about that," he said in a silky-smooth voice. "Our secretary is out on maternity leave. I'm Philip." He stretched out his hand and shook Gina's.

"Doesn't it bother you to work in an office where everyone can watch what you are doing all the time?" Gina asked.

I had tucked my hands into my pockets, instinctively avoiding the customary handshaking ritual.

Philip, noticing the lack of response, let his hand fall to his side. "Not at all," he replied with an easy smile. "Glass offices are the way of the future. They're stylish and foster a sense of openness and collaboration. Plus, the natural light exposure enhances mood and performance."

No wonder this man was a real estate agent, he sounded like a natural salesman.

"What if your butt itches?" Gina asked. "What do you do then?"

"Ignore it I guess," he said as if such a discomfort had never happened to him. "Are you looking for a home?"

"Actually, we have a family gathering coming up and we were considering renting a house," I said.

"Or two," Gina added. "We have a huge family."

"Excellent. Hotels are so impersonal these days," Philip said. "Houses will offer your family a sense of togetherness. Nothing is more important than time spent with loved ones."

I changed my mind. This guy shouldn't be a real estate agent. He should be writing greeting cards.

"Do you have a list of houses available for short-term rentals that we could review?" Gina asked. "That way we can find the ones that are close to each other and work best for us."

"Casey oversees our temporary rentals, but he's currently out of the office. I can give you his card." Philip walked over to the receptionist's desk. He riffled through one of the four cardholders, extracting a crisp card before handing it to Gina. "You can also find a list of currently available properties on our website. Unfortunately, options are pretty limited this time of year."

"We'll take a look," I replied. "But we would still like to talk about options for next year's reunion."

"Ah, that's a big one," Gina responded, her eyes lighting up with anticipation. "We're expecting thirty to fifty people to come into town for that event."

"Why don't you give me your name and number and I'll pass it on to Casey," Philip suggested.

Gina handed him a business card, and we left the office.

"Let me stop in and check my mail," Gina said as she entered the office across the hall. I waved to Francine, who was engrossed in a conversation on her headset. She waved back as we walked through the lobby.

As Gina entered her office, I could see a small pile of unopened envelopes on her desk. She began sifting through them while I pulled out my phone to text Krista and see how Sean was doing.

Moments later, three little dots danced across the screen, indicating that Krista was typing. A response popped up shortly after. "Krista says Sean's awake and wants to talk to us."

Gina, still going through her mail, tossed two of the envelopes back onto the desk, but the remaining ones made their way into the waste bin. "Let's go."

As Gina exited the building, I halted at the doorstep and cautiously searched for any signs of unwanted attention. Halfway across the pavement, Gina paused, turning back to find me still standing in the doorway.

"Chicken," she said. "You'll chase after a terrorist and face off with an arms dealer but cower in a doorway to avoid a normal guy who's interested in you."

"Bite me," I shot back as I made my way to the car.

CHAPTER 11

As Gina turned the Mustang onto Hanover Street, a white van adorned with flashing yellow lights zoomed past us. On the back of the truck, in bold green letters, it read 'Animal Control'. The van sped down the road before veering onto Lucinda's street, and a curious thrill coursed through me.

"You know we have to see what's going on," I urged.

Gina smiled as we followed the van, parking behind it near the back of Lucinda's fence.

Two men, one with Elvis Presley sideburns and the other sporting a green vest adorned with a picture of a dog in a cage on the back, emerged from the truck. Sideburns clutched a metal cage as they disappeared through the open gate of the fence, the sound of barking echoing from within. Not long after, the vest-clad guy returned to the van and withdrew a long steel pole with a metal lasso at its end.

"Shall we see what's happening?" Gina said excitedly.

As we exited the car, I noticed a tantalizing aroma of roast beef. We peered through the fence opening and were greeted by a chaotic scene. Three large dogs were frantically digging through the earth, their paws tossing clumps of grass and dirt high into the air as if searching for buried treasure. There were several noticeable bare spots scattered around the once-pristine yard that the dogs had already destroyed.

Along the fence, a large orange cat prowled as it sniffed around the flower bed. It clamped down onto a purple flower and yanked it out of the ground. The fence planks that we had moved last night were now missing entirely likely torn away by the bigger dogs in their frantic attempt to break into the yard.

On the porch, Lucinda stood near the hot tub, her voice cutting through the air as she shouted at the oblivious animals, who continued to dig and scavenge undeterred by her presence. Their fervent pursuit of the source of the enticing beef smell led them to abandon one spot for another quickly.

Gina doubled over with laughter. "This turned out so much better than I imagined in my head," she exclaimed when she finally paused to breath.

Lucinda, now visibly frustrated, hopped off the porch and stomped toward the animal control workers. "Get these filthy mongrels out of my yard!" she yelled.

Vest guy approached the multicolored black and brown dog, and reached for its collar. In a burst of energy, the dog evaded him, sprinting to the other side of the yard, where it lifted its nose to the air and inhaled deeply before choosing a new spot. It lowered its snout and sniffed the ground a few times before it started digging vigorously, dirt flying in all directions. Sideburns took hold of his pole and cautiously inched toward the largest dog in the pack, which was so big it made a lion look small.

"I don't even know how that dog fit through the hole in the fence," I remarked.

"That's a Mastiff," came from behind me.

Startled, I turned to discover Blake standing behind us. It irritated me that I didn't notice him sneaking up on us. I was trained to be mindful of my surroundings, alert to any potential threats. If I stayed in this town too much longer, I feared I might lose my edge and be forced to return to Arizona for retraining.

"What's going on in there?" Blake asked, peering through the open door. "Is someone cooking steak?"

"It seems a group of dogs have taken over Lucinda's yard," I said, gesturing towards the chaotic scene.

"Don't forget about the cat," Gina said, pointing to the orange ball of fur that had decided to tear into a cluster of pink flowers, sending petals flying like confetti.

Sideburns moved forward to place the wire lasso around the Mastiff's massive head. However, the moment the loop brushed against its ear, the dog shook its head violently, dislodging the attempt, and turned to confront Sideburn, its gaze locking onto him. A growl vibrated from deep in its throat, and it revealed its teeth, making it abundantly clear who was in charge of this situation.

Sideburns started backing up, but the dog lunged forward. The dog chased him around the yard barking, but it looked to have a smile on its face, so I wasn't sure if it was actually trying to attack the man or play with him.

They raced up onto the porch and Sideburns hit a dead end in front of the hot tub. The Mastiff barreled toward him, then skidded to a halt mere inches away. It reared up on its hind legs, stretching to its full impressive height, and placed its gigantic paws firmly on Sideburn's shoulders. The force of the impact caused the man to stumble backwards and tumbled into the hot tub with a resounding splash.

When Sideburns resurfaced, a torrent of colorful words escaped his lips. The guy in the vest rushed over to us with Lucinda hot on his heels.

"Look at what these dogs have done to my beautiful yard," she ranted at Blake. "Can't you just shoot them?" She seemed unconcerned with the man trapped in her hot tub, cornered by the now growling Mastiff who stood guard.

The young man in the vest looked irritated. "They're digging for something," he said, sniffing the air. "Have you buried trash or some type of meat in your yard?"

Lucinda's hand flew up to her throat. "How dare you insinuate something like that. This is the mayor's home. We keep it in pristine condition."

"Not anymore," Gina whispered, but not quietly enough.

Lucinda glared at her. "What are you doing here anyway? Do you two have something to do with this disaster?"

I innocently threw my hands up, palms out. "We were driving by when we saw the van and heard the barking. We stopped to see what was going on."

"I just bet," Lucinda said. "You always seem to be around when something goes wrong."

"Just lucky I guess," Gina replied, a playful smile dancing on her lips.

"I know...," Lucinda was interrupted by the black dog, who had unexpectedly shoved his nose into her backside. She yelped, jumping behind the man in the vest, her composure shattered. "Do something," she cried.

Blake shook his head, bemused, before striding away. He returned shortly, gripping a cylindrical metal whistle. He blew on the whistle, but no sound escaped.

All three dogs froze mid-action, their ears perked up. One started to whine, then all three dashed towards the larger of the two holes in the fence at breakneck speed. Within seconds they had disappeared like a criminal at a police convention.

The cat, lounging in the sun, considered the change in its surroundings. With a lazy stretch, it surveyed the now-empty yard. It must have decided it was time to leave because it leapt straight up and landed with impressive precision on the top of the fence before disappearing over the other side.

I raised an eyebrow at Blake, questioning why he was carrying a dog whistle.

"In my line of work, you often encounter aggressive dogs, so it's always best to stay one step ahead," he remarked before turning and walking away.

Lucinda huffed as she surveyed her yard, which was almost completely absent of grass. The once-vibrant flowers now lay toppled beside the flowerbed, while several large holes marred the ground, scattered unevenly across the patchy landscape.

"Guess the excitement is over," Gina said.

As we turned to leave, a scream escaped Lucinda. "There's a dead rat," she exclaimed, her eyes wide as she darted towards the flowerbed. She nudged it with her shoe, but the still form didn't move. "Get this out of here," she ordered the two animal control workers.

On the ground lay a grayish ball of fur, curled up on its side. Its long tail and legs were pink and absent of fur, and its mouth hung open, tongue lolling to the side.

Sideburns, now dripping wet from the hot tub, grabbed a shovel that was leaning against the side of the shed.

"Is that a rat?" I asked Gina. If it was, it was by far the largest I'd ever seen, including those I'd encountered in the back alleys of Pakistan.

Gina shook her head, a mischievous smile lighting up her face. "It's an opossum." She couldn't help but chuckle as she nudged me with her elbow. "Watch this."

Sideburns slid the shovel beneath the seemingly dead animal, but as soon as he attempted to lift it, the opossum's eyes popped open. It sprang to its feet and charged toward Lucinda, scrambling up her like a makeshift tree. It plastered itself against her face, wrapping its little paws around the back of her head. The tummy of the opossum pressed against her mouth, muffling her startled scream.

Sideburns couldn't help himself, he collapsed to the ground laughing.

From the sidelines, the other animal control worker sprinted over, shovel in hand, hoisting it back like a baseball bat as he zeroed in on the furry intruder. The scene was unfolding like a bad cartoon.

Fortunately, the opossum spotted the shovel and leapt off Lucinda's face before the idiot took a swing. It scurried through the smaller gap in the fence and disappeared.

Gina laughed so hard she snorted.

"This is turning out to be a wonderful day," I remarked as we walked back to the car.

* * * *

As we stepped out of the elevator at the hospital, I heard a raised female voice echo down the corridor. As we passed by the room where the screaming was coming from,

I spotted Beatrix standing defiantly in the middle of the room holding a cane above her head wielding it like a weapon. Her left leg was encased to the knee in a white plaster cast with only her toes peeking out.

Three nurses, two clad in white scrubs and one wearing navy, were trying to pacify her.

"I don't need to be here." Beatrix yelled. "I can take care of myself."

"I'm going to call your daughter right now," the nurse in the navy scrubs said as she backed out of the room leaving her colleagues to fend for themselves.

"Hurry up," Beatrix snapped, lowering her cane a fraction. "I don't want to be here all day."

I shook my head and continued walking towards Sean's room. When we entered, he was propped up in bed. His complexion was still pale, but not as ghostly as it had been the prior day. He gave us a weak smile.

"How are you feeling?" Gina asked as she rushed to his bedside, concern etched on her face.

"I have a monster headache but otherwise not too bad."

"How long have you been awake?" I asked.

"Couple of hours now. They're supposed to be taking me for another CAT scan soon," he replied, a frown appearing as he anticipated the next medical procedure.

"Have you met Bevis and Butthead?" I asked.

He smiled. "If you are referring to troopers Rhode and Grant, then yes, I had the pleasure of meeting them earlier this morning."

"I'm sure it was a pleasant experience," Krista remarked, crossing her arms over her chest.

"They weren't very pleased with the information I provided," he confessed.

"What did you tell them?" Gina probed.

"Nothing," Sean replied.

"Nothing?" I asked.

"Well almost nothing." He threw his arms up in frustration. "I can't remember a thing."

"Why don't you tell us what you do recall?" I suggested.

"Why do you want to know?" he countered, arching his eyebrow skeptically. "You're not thinking of sticking your nose in a police investigation again, are you?"

I glanced at Krista for help.

"In my cognitive psychology class, we learned that a good way to jog your memory is to think about what you did before the event that you can't remember," Krista said sitting in the chair next to the bed. She gently took his hand in hers. "Close your eyes," she instructed.

He complied.

"You told me you were going to Rita's for dinner that night," Krista continued. "What did you eat?"

"A roast beef sandwich," Sean replied.

"How did it smell?"

Sean's eyes popped open. "Like beef. Is this relevant?"

"Absolutely," Krista replied. "You need to remember every detail, no matter how small, so that you feel like you are there again. It helps make the memory vivid and alive in your mind." She slapped the back of his hand. "Now, close your eyes."

"Fine," he muttered, his eyes closing once again.

"Did you eat alone?"

"No, Officer Kline was with me."

"What did he have to eat?"

Sean's brow lifted, and a frown creased his forehead. I could almost imagine him rolling his eyes thinking that this was a waste of time, but he humored his wife. "Meatloaf and mashed potatoes."

"Was the restaurant crowded or quiet?"

There was a moment of silence while Sean contemplated the question. "No, there were only two other tables occupied, so it was quiet except for the hum of the refrigerator unit in the dessert case. We were sitting next to it."

"Excellent," Krista said, now getting excited that Sean was fully engaged in her experiment. "After dinner where did you go?"

"It was getting close to dark by then, so I got into my car to patrol town."

"Then what happened?"

"As I drove by Faukner's hardware store, I noticed two vehicles parked there: a gray sedan and a dark colored truck. Three figures stood by the cars, and the trunk was wide open. Something about the scene seemed suspicious, so I turned around to investigate."

Sean shifted in bed uncomfortably as if the memories were troublesome.

"Can you describe the men to me?" Krista asked softly, her voice filled with concern.

Sean's brow furrowed in concentration and he squeezed his eyes tight. After a long pause, he finally shook his head. "I only see black silhouettes, no faces."

The monitor next to the bed started beeping faster. I glanced at the screen, noting Sean's heart rate was increasing. It rose above one hundred twenty beats per minute. Krista exchanged a worried glance with me, and I shook my head, signaling that it was time to halt the questioning. Sean's well-being was more important than continuing the interrogation.

Krista patted his hand. "That was great, hon. That's enough for today."

Sean kept his eyes tightly shut, beads of sweat glistened on his forehead. "I want to remember," he insisted as he shook his head. "I had just shut the car door and looked at the group when one shadow pulled a gun. But I can't picture him, only the gun."

His heart rate spiked up to one forty.

Krista's face tightened with concern, the lines of worry deepening as she studied the monitor.

"That's okay," I said. "Just describe the gun."

Sean relaxed a bit as he described the gun. He said it was a black clip gun, possibly a forty-five caliber. Suddenly, his eyes flew open, and he bolted upright in bed. "I can see the hand holding the gun," he exclaimed as his heart rate shot up to one fifty. He turned to me. "The hand belongs to a white male."

At that moment a nurse in white scrubs came bursting into the room. "Mr. Wallace, you need to calm down and relax before you have a heart attack," she urged gently but firmly.

Sean leaned back against his pillow.

"I think it's time to take you for your CT scan," the nurse continued right before a man in green scrubs wheeled a stretcher into the room. "It's probably best if you leave," the nurse said to Gina and me accusingly as if it was our fault Sean's pulse elevated.

We made our way back out of the hospital, retracing our steps through the emergency room exit. As the automatic doors swished open, releasing us into the hot afternoon sun, I caught a flash of movement out of the corner of my eye. I turned my head and spotted a white-casted leg as it disappeared around the side of a nearby ambulance, whose engine was still running. 'Oh no,' I thought as I sprinted after the retreating figure.

CHAPTER 12

The driver's door slammed shut as I rounded the corner of the ambulance. Peering through the window, I could see Beatrix in the driver's seat. She was so short I could only see the top half of her head, and I wondered how she could see over the steering wheel. I tugged on the door handle but it was locked.

As I yelled for help, Beatrix squinted at me through her coke bottle glasses and a mischievous grin spread across her face, reminding me of the Grinch. With a roar, she revved the engine and in an instant the ambulance jolted forward. It barreled across the pavement and launching onto the front lawn, crashing into the 'Emergency Entrance' sign with a loud crunch.

She then swerved into the parking lot and sideswiped a silver sports car. I sprinted after her, but she floored it, straightened the wheels, and headed towards the hospital entrance without a hint of hesitation. The ambulance almost tipped onto two wheels as she made a sharp right onto the main road without even tapping the brakes.

The ambulance barely dodged a trash truck and then passed by a rubbernecker in a Buick. The trash truck swerved and hit a tree in an attempt to avoid a collision with the ambulance. The impact caused the tree to groan and crack, breaking in half and causing it to crash down on a Mercedes parked in the corner of the lot. The car alarm pierced the air as Beatrix and the ambulance vanished from sight.

There was nothing I could do but watch the disaster unfold. Just then, Gina strolled up beside me and clicked her tongue.

"Guess we're lucky we're heading in the other direction," she said.

* * * *

When we arrived in town, it was bustling with noise and people. Everyone was enthusiastic about the grand reenactment set to end in just two days. On our way, Willy had called Gina to let her know that her boat was ready and waiting for her at the dock. Gina was excited to take it for its first test drive since she inherited it. Her energy was so high that I had to promise her we would take it out after we were finished in town.

I slipped on my sunglasses and stationed myself at the corner of the square in front of the bank to observe the scene. The bank would be closed for the days of the reenactment because this crazy town treated it as a holiday. In contrast, the surrounding buildings on the square housed quaint shops and restaurants that would stay open and be bustling with business.

In one corner of the square, a sturdy wooden platform had been erected. This makeshift stage stood two feet above the ground and was large enough to hold the vice president and at least half a dozen Secret Service agents. I had to laugh at the irony that it probably took the better part of two days to erect the platform that the vice president would use for ten minutes.

"Secret Service agents will be with the Vice President and scattered throughout the crowd," I said. "Besides, it would be nearly impossible to take a shot at him from the crowd. Someone would spot the gun."

Gina nodded. "They'll sweep the area around the platform for bombs. If there is an abandoned box or even a backpack left in the crowd, they'll spot that too."

I shielded my eyes with my hand and scanned the rooftops of the surrounding buildings. "The most ideal location for a shooter would be across the square on the rooftop of the hotel."

Gina pointed at the hotel. "Someone could easily slip open one of the windows and shoot from their room without anyone being the wiser."

I frowned as I considered her words. She was absolutely right. The hotel was six stories tall with at least two dozen windows facing in the direction where the speech would take place. We hurried across the street to the grassy area at the center of the square.

Gina rummaged through her purse and retrieved Pap's map, her fingers unfolding the creased paper. I grabbed hold of two corners as we spread it out between us, scrutinizing its details against the buildings ahead, seeking any clues or vantage points we might have overlooked.

"According to this map, the buildings in the square are at least one level higher than the adjacent buildings," I said, tracing a finger along the lines. "That elevation will make it harder for anyone to traverse the roofs from one building to the next."

Gina nodded. "With the right equipment, it could be possible. And let's not underestimate the crowd. There's a good chance that someone in the crowd would spot someone climbing a rope to a higher roof. I'd bet there will be at least one roof that a government sniper will be stationed."

As she spoke, my gaze caught movement above. I glanced up and spotted a figure clad in camouflage standing on the hotel roof. He was speaking with another man dressed in a black suit.

I nodded at Gina, urging her to follow my line of sight. "It seems they're already planning to station someone on the hotel roof, which is the tallest building in the square."

From up there he had a clear view of everything below. A shadow from behind fell over the map, blocking out the sun. I turned and spotted a man standing behind us, his gaze fixed intently on our map.

Despite the sweltering heat from the hottest part of the day during the hottest part of the year, he was dressed in a pair of sleek black pants paired with a matching windbreaker. The jacket was only zipped enough to hide the gun that rested in a holster at his side, which I knew was there because I spotted the telltale bulge. His eyes were hidden behind reflective sunglasses, which were standard issue for government operatives. There was no doubt in my mind that he was part of the presidential detail.

"Is there something I can help you ladies find?" he asked with an edge in his tone.

Great. Here we were, potentially dealing with a sniper lurking nearby, and he thought we looked suspicious. Of course, we were the only ones standing in the center of the square holding a large map and scrutinizing the rooftops. Even with Gina in her hot pink 'I love Gettysburg' tourist shirt, we still managed to stand out from the throngs of visitors. Ironic considering I was trained to blend seamlessly into the background, not to attract attention.

Gina looked the agent up and down, a playful smile on her lips. "How about a date?"

His expression remained flat and unchanged, showing he was not amused.

I elbowed her. "We were looking for the statue of Lincoln."

He stared at us, at least I thought he did, as his mirrored glasses obscured any glimpse of his eyes. After a moment, he pointed towards his right, where the majestic Lincoln Statue stood a mere thirty feet away. It was surrounded by tourists snapping photos.

I pulled my blonde card and thumped my forehead with my palm. "How could we have missed it?" I said, quickly refolding the map.

Gina gave a fake girly-sounding giggle. "Thank you, cutie."

I grabbed her arm and hauled her across the bustling street. As we waited in line for our turn to get our pictures taken with Lincoln, I stole a glance at the agent. He was standing in the square, his legs firmly apart and hands clasped together in front of him, gazing in our direction. After a few seconds, he raised two fingers to his ear, likely trying to cut through the crowd's chatter to hear the voice coming through his earpiece. He listened intently for a brief moment before turning and walking away.

We decided to stay in line, keenly aware that we might still be under surveillance. When it was finally Gina's turn, she hugged the imposing statue from the side, wrapping her leg around its waist. Leaning in, she planted a quick peck on its cheek before spinning around to strike another pose. She leaned over and rubbed her backside against the cold metal.

"Are you quite finished molesting Lincoln?" I asked, trying to stifle my laughter as I watched her antics.

Gina and I navigated through the mob of people.

"It's like walking through the streets of Delhi," I remarked, glancing around at the sea of people.

"Now, you're exaggerating. No place is as crowded as India," Gina replied.

As we stepped inside the hotel, we were greeted by the grandeur of the lobby. The area was adorned with gray marble floors that shimmered under the glow of the lights, while the walls were painted a warm beige. To our left stood a polished concierge desk, and to the right, a large arched entryway to the restaurant where the sound of chatter floated through the air. Flanking the entrance were two large planters filled with flowers, giving the room a pop of color and filling it with their fresh floral scent.

Approaching the desk, we were greeted by a sharply dressed concierge. He wore a meticulously buttoned white shirt with navy stripes and flawlessly pressed khaki pants that were without a single wrinkle. Even the white ascot wrapped around his neck was wrinkle-free. To be honest, I hadn't seen an ascot on a man since Freddy from the Scooby-Doo cartoon I watched as a child, despite my years living in Europe.

As we stepped closer, he beamed at us. "Welcome to the Gettysburg Inn. How may I help you?"

"We would like a room for the night," Gina said. "Preferably one that faces the street."

The concierge cast us a look of disbelief, as if we dared to wear white after Labor Day. "That's simply not possible," he said in a snotty tone. "Rooms at this hotel are booked a year in advance, especially for this week."

"Okay," Gina said. "Our friend Daniel Craig is staying here, so we'll just go visit him."

It was evident by the look he gave Gina that he was unaware that one of the guests had used such a familiar name to check in. If he didn't think we were crazy before, he most certainly did now.

"I'm sorry, but with the Vice President visiting, we have heightened security protocols in place," he replied. "No one is allowed on the room floors except registered guests."

"Let's get something to eat at the restaurant," I suggested to Gina. "We'll call Daniel and have him meet us there."

"Tell him I loved him in Casino Royal," the concierge said with a smug smile. It was evident from his scrutinizing gaze that he doubted our ability to afford a meal at the hotel's overpriced establishment.

We slipped inside the restaurant and stood against the wall, positioning ourselves out of sight.

"We've got to get upstairs to check out those rooms," Gina said.

"We need a distraction," I replied, my mind racing with possibilities

"On it." Gina's eyes sparkled as she rummaged through her bottomless purse.

"No way. Under no circumstances do you get to blow something up." The Secret Service would lock us up for life.

She smiled. "You're no fun. I'm just looking for my phone."

"I hope we're never in a real crisis and need to navigate through that abyss of a bag you call a purse," I grumbled, pulling my phone from my pocket. "I'll handle this."

I dialed the number, and as soon as the call connected, I spoke quickly. "We need a distraction. Can you help us out?" I gave her our location.

"What kind of distraction do you need?" Genesis asked, the sound of her gum cracking was audible through the phone. I could hear several dogs barking in the background. I gave her a rundown of our situation.

"That's got to be Marcus at the desk," She replied. "I got this. Be there shortly."

We waited inside the entryway ready to act as soon as the path was clear.

Genesis arrived wearing a pastel purple jumpsuit resembling an Easter egg, carrying a large brown leather purse. With a graceful stride, she made her way to the reception desk, her purse thudding softly against the polished wood as she set it down on the corner near the front door.

I couldn't catch the whispered conversation between her and the concierge, but suddenly a head popped out of the purse, grabbing the concierge's attention. Without warning, a small dog leaped out of the purse. It was supposed to be a white dog, but its paws and legs were splattered with caked on mud.

The concierge recoiled, his wide eyes fixed on the lively creature as he instinctively raised his hands in front of him. His voice rose a few octaves, a mix of disbelief and alarm, catching the notice of the elevator operator nearby.

Taking that as our cue, Gina and I decided to make a hasty escape towards the stairs. As we hurried past the elevator, I heard the concierge shout in a flustered tone, "No pets are allowed in this hotel!" Just as the words left his mouth, the muddy dog ran to him and placed its paws on his pristine shirt, eliciting a high-pitched girlie scream.

Gina and I disappeared into the stairwell, closing the door quietly behind us. Since there were no rooms on the first floor, we would have to go up three flights of stairs to get to the third floor. When we arrived at our destination, I cracked the door open to peer out into the hallway.

The walls were the same boring beige as the lobby, with faded carpet that muffled our footsteps as we stepped into the corridor. No one was in sight, so we emerged from the stairwell and stopped in front of room 311.

"Craig's room will be facing the square," Gina stated.

I knocked on the door.

"Housekeeping," Gina blurted out.

"Really?" I shot back.

"We have to say something," she insisted.

"And when he opens the door and we don't have fresh towels in our hands?"

Gina's gaze darted around, searching for an imaginary cleaning cart. "Oh, yeah. I didn't think that through," she admitted.

Luckily, no one answered the door. I quickly removed my lock picks from my boot, and within a few moments, I heard the lock unbolt.

"Good thing this hotel hasn't upgraded to key card locks," I remarked.

"Guess they want to maintain some of the historic charm." As soon as we entered the room, I walked past the king-size bed in the middle of the room to the large, elegant curtains, parting them to let in the warm sunlight that poured through the expansive picture window. Gina, on the other hand, seemed drawn to the bed. She sat on the edge, bouncing lightly to check its stability. Then she decided to climb onto the bed, jumping up and down with abandon like a small child.

"I always wanted to jump on someone else's bed," she said.

"Jumping on a bed, leaping out of a belfry, it's quite a week of firsts for you," I replied. "But seriously, can you focus for a moment and search the room for weapons?" Gina sighed but crawled off the bed. I turned my attention to the window, examining the glass. I pushed against it, feeling the rigid steel letting me know these windows weren't meant to be opened, they were completely sealed shut. I inspected the corners where the glass met the wall, tapping gently on the glass.

"This glass is at least half an inch thick," I observed, running my finger along its smooth surface. "It would take a tremendous amount of force to break it," I paused. "Not to mention the amount of noise it would create. Half the hotel would hear if someone tried to shatter it."

"Don't forget the people on the street below," Gina added, closing the closet door. "It's probably designed that thick so no suicidal people can jump out of the window," she continued, bending down to peer under the bed. "After all, people plummeting to their deaths is bad for hotel business." She straightened up brushing off her hands. "No weapons here, not even a screwdriver." She grinned, giving me a knowing look, and I knew she was recalling an incident I had with a screwdriver.

I recalled the man I had killed with one. "He deserved it. He was trafficking women."

Just then, I heard the metallic sound of a key turning in the lock. The door swung open revealing a balding man holding the hand of a woman at least half his age. Their cheerful smiles vanished abruptly as they spotted us, and he dropped her hand quickly.

"Who are you?" he inquired.

Gina stepped forward. "We housekeeping," she said in a thick fake foreign accent using a dialect I'd never heard before.

"I'm the housekeeping supervisor," I added. "I was here inspecting Carmen's work. This is unacceptable," I said, turning to address Gina. "Look at that bed. The bedspread is supposed to be neat and smooth. Instead, it looks like someone has been jumping up and down on it." I pointed out the now wrinkled comforter.

"So sorry," she replied in her broken English.

"You're demoted to laundry duty. Head down to the washing machines." Gina lowered her gaze and walked past the couple and out of the room.

"I'll send a new maid up immediately," I assured the couple.

The woman ran her fingers down the man's arm.

"Um, that won't be necessary," he said as he gestured for me to leave. Without hesitating, he placed a "Do not disturb" sign on the door before closing it.

I found Gina waiting at the entrance to the stairwell.

"Did you notice his wedding band and the absence of one on her finger?" I remarked.

"So, the fake Daniel Craig isn't a terrorist just an adulterer."

"It seems so," I replied, bouncing down the stairs. When we reached the lobby, we glanced straight ahead and moved with purpose as if we belonged in the hotel. Genesis was nowhere in sight, and the concierge was engaged with a couple at the front desk. Unfortunately, he spotted us and his head snapped up.

"Wait a moment," he shouted after us, as he swiftly rounded the corner of the desk. Gina and I quickened our pace, weaving through the throngs of people on the street before he could reach the door. We disappeared into the nearest alley.

"Can we go try out my boat now?" Gina asked.

Given that we hadn't uncovered a single thread of evidence to substantiate my theory, I didn't see why not.

CHAPTER 13

We decided to make a stop at the candy store for snacks and drinks. Luckily, the store was more of a general store than a basic candy store. You could buy the essentials you needed to stock your pantry, along with a wide variety of candies.

I chose an apple from a nearby stand and made my way to the wall cooler, pulling out two chilled bottles of water. As I closed the door, I spotted Luke at the adjacent cooler reaching for a case of beer.

"Hi," he greeted me. "How are you?"

"Good. Are you getting some supplies?"

"Liam and I are having a few friends over tonight," he said.

"Is Liam around, too? I hadn't seen him yet."

Luke shrugged. "He's around here somewhere."

I nodded. "Talk to you later," I said, turning away to find Gina.

I spotted her in line for the register, holding a bag filled with colorful, oversized candy, each about the size of a quarter.

"They're jaw breakers," Gina said.

"Didn't I see somewhere that these things explode when left out in the hot sun?"

Gina's eyes lit up. "Really?" she said excitedly.

"Never mind." I sighed, realizing that this was just what we needed, another object she could cause havoc with.

We stood in line and waited for our turn to check out. I couldn't quite see the person at the register because a blue ball cap obscured their face. But I saw the clerk hand them their change. As the person reached for their bag, the short sleeve of their shirt slid up their arm, revealing the lower half of a tattoo of with curved dagger piercing a heart.

"There," I said to Gina, pointing as I began to weave through the line of people towards the front. The commotion of me trying to get through the crowd must have alerted the person at the front because the figure in the blue ball cap vanished from view. I looked around and spotted the blue cap darting through the sliding glass doors. I tossed my water and apple on the conveyor belt and sprinted outside, scanning the area for any sign of the disappearing figure.

I ran down the sidewalk, my mind racing as I caught sight of the blue cap moving quickly around the corner. Two blocks away from the store, a sharp crack shattered the air. A gunshot rang out about fifty yards ahead. I sprinted half the distance before diving behind a bench for cover.

My pulse kicked up as I went into mission mode. Everything around me faded into a dull roar. My focus sharpened, tuning out the crowd that seemed unaware of the danger. Two more shots rang out, prompting me to reach my hand behind me, my fingers gripping my gun. Just as I was ready to pull it out of my waistband, I felt a hand pressing down on my shoulder, jolting me from my concentration.

"Wait," Gina said from behind me, her gaze fixed intently down the street. I peered over the wooden bench and spotted two men dressed in blue Civil War Union uniforms, each gripping a rifle. As I stood up, I noticed two other men sprawled in the middle of the road, clad in dusty gray uniforms. I shook my head and scanned the area for the blue baseball hat that was now gone. I sighed. Only in Gettysburg could a staged shooting interrupt the apprehension of a real criminal.

"What did you see?" Gina asked.

I recounted my observation in the grocery store. "It was definitely a man's arm," I said as we strolled down the street towards the reenactment, veering away from the crowd that had gathered to watch.

"Wasn't Liam wearing a blue ball cap in the hardware store the other day?"

I nodded. "We may have to keep a closer eye on those two brothers. We should stay in town and look for him."

Gina's bottom lip protruded, and she gave me puppy dog eyes, her go-to when she wanted something.

"Fine, we'll go see your boat, but just a short ride."

Suddenly, the creaky door of one of the oldest houses on the block flew open and a woman in a long-sleeved white cotton dress that covered her completely down to her ankles dashed onto the street, stopping right in front of Gina and me.

"They shot my daughter," she yelled to the crowd.

"We'll handle this, ma'am," a union officer said as he walked past her and into the house, the onlookers following in his wake.

As the woman in the Civil War dress turned back toward us, a sinking feeling settled in my stomach. It was my mother. Her face was red and perspiration covered her brow, as her eyes flared with recognition. "This was the part you were supposed to play," she spat as she turned and stormed off back to the house, the crowd parting before her.

"Aren't you glad we didn't volunteer now?" Gina asked as we continued down the street.

"More than you realize."

We were just about to cross through the town square when I caught sight of the hotel concierge standing atop the staircase of the hotel, deep in conversation with the Secret Service agent we had encountered earlier. The concierge gestured animatedly towards the crowd as he talked.

"We should head down the alley," I urged.

Gina followed my gaze before quickly agreeing. As we took the narrow alley leading back to the car, I couldn't help but chuckle at the irony of the situation. Here we were, two presumed civilians, while at least one member of a terrorist organization lurked in town, and somehow, Gina and I had found ourselves on the Secret Service's watch list.

As we headed out of town, my cellphone chimed. It was Pap. He had received some information about the VP's arrival and was at Gina's house waiting for us.

Upon arrival, we found him sitting on the porch swing with a rolled-up document in his hand.

"Why didn't you just go inside and wait for us?" Gina asked.

"I'll leave the breaking and entering to you two," He replied, winking while rocking gently in the swing.

"We haven't broken into anything this week," I said.

"Yet." Gina felt a need to add.

We headed into the kitchen to have a private conversation without any neighbors eavesdropping.

"Do you have any coffee?" Pap asked as he sat down at the table.

I moved to the counter. "What did you find out?" I asked as I poured water into the coffee pot.

"The Vice President is flying in shortly before the event starts," he said.

"So, he won't be staying in town," I said.

"He isn't even driving up from DC?" Gina added.

Pap shook his head. "His car arrived last night and is currently at the marine reserve camp at the edge of town. He'll be flying into Gettysburg airport, and the plan is for the caravan to leave the base and meet him there. After that, they'll head into town for him to deliver his speech then right back to the airport."

"The town is secure," I remarked, my nail tapping rhythmically against the surface of the counter as I pondered the situation. "If I were planning an attack, I would aim for the Vice President during his route to town."

"Let's not overlook the possibility that they're planning a bombing with mass casualties," Gina interjected.

"I think I agree with Sydney," Pap said. "I talked to General Marshall earlier today, and he assured me that the town has been thoroughly swept. They even cleaned out the basements of the buildings near the square. Sharpshooters are already stationed on the rooftop of the hotel, and undercover agents are blending into the crowds. Not to mention a few bomb sniffing canines. Security is so tight that they'd spot a tick on a dog."

General Marshall was one of the highest-ranking officers in the army, and last I heard, he was set to receive his third star. The aroma of freshly brewed coffee filled the air as the coffee machine dinged. I poured three cups and made my way over to the table.

"This is the map of the marine camp." Pap opened the document in his hand and rolled it out onto the table. We used our coffee cups to hold down the corners. "There are only a few active-duty Marines on it. It's mostly used for reserve units now."

"Where did you get a map of the inside of a military base?" I asked. Military bases were top-secret government facilities and weren't open to public access.

"Does it matter?" he asked. "The base covers twenty-five acres and has six main buildings. The vehicle is sitting in the middle of this parking lot." Pap tapped the spot on the maps beside the furthest building inside the base.

"I assume there is no easy way to get to the car while it is at the base?" I asked, picking up my cup of coffee, causing the corner of the map to roll up.

Pap shook his head again. Before I could take a sip of my coffee, he removed the cup from my hand, flattened the map back out, and placed it back in its original location. "The camp is surrounded by eight-foot-tall wire fencing with barbed wire at the top. On one side, there is a neighborhood of houses, and the other side and the back of the base border the state forest preserve land.

Gina frowned. "The best way to follow the VP's movement is to track him."

"No way you can put a tracer on the vehicle without raising alarms and getting caught breaking onto the base," Pap pointed out. "Besides, I'm sure they'll scan the vehicle before it leaves their gates again, just in case they missed anything during the last check."

I picked up my cup to take a drink, causing the map to roll up again. "We could follow it with a drone. That way we'd know exactly when the vehicle left the base." I said, taking a sip of the aromatic brew. "Gina, do you have one?"

Gina shook her head. "No, drone, but I did just finish upgrading an RC car. I souped up the motor and added-"

I raised my hand to interrupt her. "We don't have time to talk about an RC car."

I unrolled the map again, pressing it down with my palm. "Are there any parking lots for hiking trails near the Marine camp?"

"There's a parking lot about a half mile down the road from the base where hikers go all the time, "Pap replied. "The path connects to the Appalachian Trail further up the mountain."

"Hang on a second," I said as I ran out of the room. In my bedroom, I grabbed my duffel bag and upended it onto the bed, spilling out the remainder of the contents. There wasn't much left inside since I had already removed my clothes and laptop. I traveled light, but to my delight, I found a few remnants from my last mission scattered among the items. My partner must have forgotten to empty the bag before sending it back to the States after the accident.

I pushed aside the faded army green sweatshirt and matching fatigue pants, and a few things the government would frown upon if they knew I still possessed them. I smiled when I spotted the black plastic box sitting underneath. I grabbed it and headed back downstairs.

"I got it," I announced as I deposited the box on the table. As I lifted the lid, I revealed a small handheld gadget that resembled a smartphone, along with four small silver-colored balls the size of marbles.

Gina picked up one of the balls and rolled it around between her fingers. "What are these?"

"Paintballs," I replied. "They're left over from my last mission. Curtis forgot to clean out my duffel bag."

A perplexed expression crossed Pap's face. "And their special why?"

"They're filled with mercury and some other radioactive chemical I can't remember."

Gina dropped the ball back into the case. "Isn't mercury poisonous?" she asked, examining her fingers as if she expected them to start blistering and melt off.

"The mercury is contained inside the plastic shell, so I don't think you're going to die," I said. "At least not today." I picked up the handheld device. "This is a tracker that traces the radioactive material. It's effective up to two miles away. We can go through the forest and sneak up to the perimeter of the fence far enough away not to be noticed. The silver in the paintball matches the color of vehicle wheels, making it virtually undetectable."

Pap examined one of the balls. "The scanning device they use for trackers relies on radio waves or electrical computer chips. They won't pick up radioactive elements. Very clever, I assume you've employed these tactics before?"

I nodded. "All we need is a paintball gun with a scope."

"My... supplier can get us one," Gina said. She pulled her phone out of her purse, and her fingers flew across the screen with a series of clicks.

"Is this the same supplier who obtained the illegal police radio for you?" I asked.

"Maybe," she replied. Her phone emitted the distinctive swoosh signaling the message had been sent.

Now I was worried.

After a moment, her phone dinged. "He said he'll have it in a couple of hours." She slipped her phone back into her purse. "Plenty of time for us to take the boat for a spin."

Pap rolled up the map and left it on the table. "I'll keep you posted if I hear anything else."

We followed him out the door.

* * * *

We turned off the main road and drove down a single-lane gravel road for about a mile. Finally, the trees parted, and we pulled into a small parking lot. The creek with a dock was in front of us, with the rest of the lot surrounded by trees, and not a single other vehicle was in the lot.

As we pulled up in front of the long wooden dock, I took in the scene. The dock itself was wide, about ten feet across, with a weathered appearance hinting at the years of exposure to the elements. At one end was a boat launch with a concrete ramp that disappeared under the water. At the other end there were two half-circular metal bars glistening in the sun, indicating a ladder. There were two boats secured to the dock.

Gina's boat was tied at the end of a pier that jutted out from the center of the dock. The wind danced across the water, creating ripples which produced a lapping sound against the wooden structure.

As soon as my foot touched the pier, I realized that, unlike the dock that ran along the shore, the pier wasn't secured to the ground. It bobbed up and down with the waves and tilted slightly when I stepped onto it. Gina, unaware of this, jumped onto the pier with both feet. It dipped, causing her to lose her balance. She dropped to her knees, reaching out to steady herself against the boards. The pier moaned and creaked, and if it weren't for the fact that a few of the rotting boards had been replaced with new ones,

I would have thought the pier was completely unmaintained and ready to fall apart. I was still questioning the chance of a board breaking and falling through into the murky water.

"Are you sure about this?" I asked.

"I'm good," Gina replied, as she cautiously stood back up, arms out to her side like a tight rope walker. "I didn't realize that it was a floating pier."

We walked down the swaying structure toward Gina's boat. The vessel was an old model, looking like it was left over from the seventies. Its aluminum frame had a faded and peeling orange stripe down the side. At the front was a captain's chair elevated two feet above the top of the boat on a metal pole like a barber chair. The seat was upholstered in the ugliest shade of brown vinyl that ever existed, and it had a long piece of green duct tape that crisscrossed the center, most likely covering a tear.

A small engine was at the front of the boat, looking so old I doubted it functioned. In contrast, a brand-new engine was mounted at the back. In front of it was a bench seat in the same hideous brown color as the captain's chair. There was no traditional steering wheel; instead, a handle protruded from the front of the engine for steering, leaving me wondering just how proficient Gina was. The boat was secured to the pier by two metal T-shaped fittings, one at the front and the other at the back.

"Do you even know how to drive a boat?" I asked.

"How hard can it be?" Gina replied, tossing our grocery bag of treats into the boat. "Turn the handle left to steer left, turn it right to go right. Simple." She walked to the back of the boat and started untying the knot that secured it to the pier. "Unhook the front."

I wasn't sure about her logic, but with my complete lack of experience operating a boat, I decided it was better not to argue. I untied the front of the boat and hopped onboard.

"Hurry up," I said as my end of the craft started drifting further away from the pier.

"It's tight. I bet it's a sailor's knot," she replied. "Do I look like someone who knows how to untie a sailor's knot?"

By the time she managed to unhook it, the end of the boat had already drifted a foot away from the pier. When she got it untied, she placed one foot on the boat. Just then, a gust of wind blew, causing the boat to lurch and sway unsteadily.

With her arms flailing in an attempt to regain her balance, the boat pulled further from the dock. "Uh oh," Gina said as she stood there with her feet separated into a split that would have impressed an Olympic gymnast. I had taken a step towards her when her legs finally gave out and she fell into the water with a resounding splash.

I sighed as I grabbed the rope and jumped back onto the pier so the boat wouldn't float away. I looked down and saw little bubbles seconds before her head broke through the surface as she coughed and cursed at the same time. I reattached the rope to the pier, glancing over to see her doggie paddling in place.

"Help me up," she called as she made her way to the end of the pier.

I looked at her with a bemused expression. "You want me to deadlift you, along with an extra thirty pounds of wet clothes, straight up onto this pier? I don't think so." I pointed to the dock. "There's a ladder at the end down there. Swim over and I'll meet you."

I jogged down the pier and dock to where the ladder awaited.

"Hold on a second, let me move this cloth." There was a green piece of fabric intertwined with the ladder.

I bent down and tugged on the material, but it didn't move. "It must really be stuck." I shifted my weight to get better leverage. As I tugged harder, I was able to drag it up and was surprised when I realized it wasn't a random piece of floating material after all.

CHAPTER 14

"Crap," I said as the back of a man's head broke the surface.

"What is it?" Gina asked as she swam closer, spotting the green shirt.

"A dead body," I replied as I tugged it a little further out of the water, causing the back and an arm to break the surface.

"Eeew," Gina said as she quickly started to paddle away, splashing me in the process.

"You're such a baby," I said.

She raised her arm above the surface of the water in an attempt to give me the finger, but it only caused her head to slip back under the water.

"I can't lift it here," I said. "I'm going to push it toward the shore and we can lift it out there." I descended the ladder two rungs and felt the cool water creep over the tops of my boots.

"Count me out," Gina shouted as she swam ten feet away and headed towards the shore.

I grabbed the back of the shirt and one arm and pushed the body towards the shore. I could feel the water squishing between my toes with every step, as I walked down the wooden dock to the point where it met the shore.

"You are going to help me tow it out," I told Gina.

"You should be able to do it, you don't have to deadlift it straight up onto the dock."

I shot her a withering glare.

"Fine," she relented, as she trudged over to me. "But I'm heading straight home for a hot shower as soon as we're done."

"Don't worry," I said, grabbing the body under an armpit. "All the dead body cooties already washed off into the water you were swimming in."

She stuck her tongue out at me as she grabbed the other side. We hauled it out of the water until only its legs were still in the creek. We turned the body over to find that his throat had been slit open.

"Doesn't take a brain surgeon to figure out how he died," Gina said.

The dead guy appeared to be in his early thirties with brown hair. "Do you recognize him?" I asked.

Gina shook her head. I gripped his arm to tug him further out of the water when something caught my eye. I rolled up his shirt sleeve and spotted the familiar heart and dagger tattoo on his inner arm.

Gina whistled. "Do you think he's the guy from the grocery store?"

"I don't know." I studied the tattoo for a moment. "Something's not right with this."

Gina leaned over to inspect the tattoo, making sure not to touch the body again.

"It's missing the word justice on the handle," I continued.

"It also looks like a different pattern on the handle," she added. "Is it from a different terrorist group?"

"No," I said, letting the arm slip from my grasp. I gazed out over the water, my mind racing to connect the dots. I started pacing on the shoreline. "The terrorists were likely using this poor guy for their own dark purposes. He probably noticed the tattoo on the arm of the real terrorists and thought if he got one himself, it might give him acceptance." I came to a halt as I stood before the lifeless body.

"That's why the tattoo looks different," Gina said. "The real terrorists were just manipulating him, planning on eliminating him as soon as he no longer served a purpose."

"Exactly," I replied. "And since they didn't know about the tattoo, they didn't know to remove it when they killed him."

"But why kill him here and throw the body in the water?"

"I don't know." I leaned down to examine the tattoo more closely. "Look at the inflamed redness of the skin surrounding it. It almost appears sunburned."

"It seems like the skin is scabbed and seeping."

Pulling out my phone, I snapped several pictures. "I don't think this tattoo is that old. Maybe a week at the most."

"Maybe if we visit the local tattoo parlor, we'll find the artist who applied it, and they can supply the guy's name."

After dialing 911, we sat on the dock and waited for the cops to arrive. I untied my boots and removed them, then peeled off my socks to wring out the excess water.

Gina glanced at the inconspicuous little pocket integrated into the side of my left boot. "Won't the water rust your lock picks?"

I shook my head. "A friend of mine in Japan made them for me. They're titanium."

Gina's eyebrow shot up. "Is this the same friend who handcrafted your special pocketknife?"

I nodded. My knife wasn't an ordinary pocketknife; it was a work of art, equipped with a few extra features that made it invaluable to me. That's why I carried it everywhere.

It didn't take long for the first patrol car to come barreling into the lot, lights flashing and siren blaring. It was followed closely by the black, unmarked car, which I recognized as Blake's.

"It's getting to the point that when I hear about a dead body, my mind automatically jumps to you," Blake said as he walked over to us.

"As in your suggesting I'm going to be the next dead body?" I shot back.

He crossed his arms over his chest and frowned.

"Fine, we came here to take a ride on Gina's boat," I said. "We weren't expecting to find a dead body floating in the water."

"Yet here you are," Blake replied.

"Maybe I spend all day driving around town looking for a dead body just so I can see you again," I said sarcastically.

Blake fought not to smile but couldn't resist. "There are better ways to get my attention." Blake glanced at Gina, who still had water droplets dripping off the end of her hair. "Fall in?" he asked, not looking at all surprised.

She glared at him.

He swiftly collected our statements before going over to the two officers positioned near the body who were waiting for the coroner to arrive.

"Do you think the state troopers will show up?" Gina asked.

"They're unaware that this is linked to Sean's case, so not likely."

"Let's get out of here just in case," she replied.

* * * *

We headed straight home so Gina could get a shower and, I quote, "scrub the ickiness from the dead body off." I changed into my green fatigue pants and my matching green T-shirt. If we were going to sneak up to the marine camp, I wanted to blend in as much as possible. Gina emerged wearing black leggings and a brown T-shirt.

I raised an eyebrow.

"I don't own anything green anymore," she declared. "I tossed it all out when I left the army. I figured I had worn enough green for a lifetime. Besides, green is not a good color for my complexion."

I rolled my eyes. "So, you're trying to pass for a deer in the woods?"

"I was thinking more along the lines of a tree."

Her phone buzzed. She glanced at the screen, then informed me that the paintball gun was ready.

As we pulled into the driveway of her alleged dealer, I recognized the place immediately. The place was Terrance Christman's, AKA Church. He was an ex-Marine who had a motorcycle shop in his garage. The garage door stood open, revealing him hunched over a Harley.

As we approached, he paused in his work and nodded at us. He tossed the wrench that was in his hand onto the workbench, where it landed with a clang.

"Your supplies are in the back," he said, stepping around the bike before making his way towards a door in the back wall.

"Supplies?" I asked Gina, wondering about the use of the plural since we were only picking up a paintball gun, but she walked past me without answering.

Church flipped on the light switch, illuminating the interior and revealing an unexpected sight that had me frozen in the doorway. Two walls were lined with gun racks. Each filled with different types of rifles standing vertically like soldiers at attention. The third wall housed a long glass display case filled with an assortment of handguns and knives.

"They're legal," he said, taking in my shocked expression. "I'm a registered gun shop." He walked behind the gun case. "Paintball rifles aren't usually equipped with scopes," he continued, bending to retrieve a weapon from the floor. "So, it took me a bit to attach one and site it." He placed a black paintball rifle on the top of the counter that, if I didn't know better, I would have thought was a real firearm. "It should be accurate up to fifty yards."

"I was thinking more like a hundred," I replied, picking up the rifle and peering down the scope.

He let out a slow whistle. "What kind of course are you going to that you need a hundred-yard accuracy?"

"Doesn't matter," I replied, removing the paintball clip so I could inspect it closely.

Church shook his head, then he produced two army-green metal cylinders, each about half the length of a spray can. Their tops had a distinctive grenade-like design.

"Your other item is in back," he said before exiting through a doorway behind him.

I eyed Gina with concern when she dropped the two grenades into her purse.

"Don't worry," she said when she saw the look on my face. "They're just flash grenades."

Flash grenades were non-lethal devices known for eliciting a bright flash of light and a loud bang when detonated. Police used them to disorient individuals before capture.

"Here you go," Church said when he returned with a black box. The top half featured a screen with a small microphone attached to it.

"It took some digging, but I managed to track down a buddy who hooked me up with one. Not sure why you need an ETD, though?"

"ETD?" An ETD, or Explosive Trace Detector, was precisely what it sounded like. It was designed to sniff out elements used in bomb-making.

"Later," Gina replied, as she scooped up her new acquisitions from the counter. "Charge me," she called over her shoulder before exiting the shop.

As we headed down the road towards the tattoo parlor, I asked about the ETD.

"Don't spaz out, but I had a thought," Gina said.

"Why is my skin all of a sudden starting to itch?"

"Ha, ha," she said, turning onto Baltimore Street. "I was thinking it wouldn't be a bad idea to take another look at the car the dead guy was in."

"You mean the one sitting in the police impound?"
She nodded.

"The impound lot surrounded by a ten-foot chain link fence that possibly has surveillance cameras and most likely two snarling Rottweilers?"

"I have wire cutters and dog biscuits."

I sliced my hand through the air dismissively. "No way! You're out of your mind."

"Don't you think it would be beneficial to sneak a look inside for any clues? This ETD doesn't just detect bomb making chemicals, it's sensitive enough to detect gunpowder residue too."

"Don't you think the police have already gone through the vehicle?"

"Not thoroughly enough," she countered. "You know how they are. They overlook the small details and miss evidence that we've been trained to find. They're focused on clues related to the murder, but they don't realize we're dealing with something far worse."

"It's a bad idea."

"So, you're not even going to think about it?" she said with a pout on her lips.

"Fine, I suppose I can think about it," I replied. "But only as a last resort, like if an alien force invades Earth and wipes out all law enforcement."

Her face brightened. "As long as you consider it."

* * * *

The tattoo shop was in the heart of town, down a quiet side street. The sign on the front had a picture of a skull being shot out of a black cannon with the name 'D-Dog Tattoos' underneath.

When we entered the shop, the first thing that hit me was the tangy scent of incense. I could hear a soft, continuous buzzing sound like a bumblebee when it flies past your head, coming from the back of the shop. The walls were painted a vibrant violet, with framed photos showcasing popular tattoo designs. There were black and white skulls, as well as colorful roses and dragons.

Behind the reception desk stood a young woman, wearing black lipstick that perfectly matched her long black hair. "I'm Kena. Can I help you find a tattoo?"

"Not today," I replied, approaching the desk.

"What's that smell?" Gina asked. "I like it."

"Lemongrass incense, it's the customer's favorite."

"We wanted to ask you about a tattoo a friend of ours has," I said. "We have a picture." I turned my phone screen towards her.

She squinted at the image before turning around and yelling, "D-dog, some women are here to see you." She pivoted back towards us. "I don't tattoo. I work the desk."

"Are they IRS?" came a deep male voice.

"No, they have a picture they want you to look at."

"Send them back," he instructed over the continuous buzzing sound.

Kena nodded her head towards an open doorway.

As we made our way through the doorway, the buzzing intensified. Inside the room was a large man sitting in a black leather chair that resembled a barber's chair. He had a long gray ponytail and a beard to match. He was wearing leather chaps and a leather vest that resembled the attire of a biker.

His arm was in the midst of receiving a tattoo from a man perched on a rolling chair beside him. The artist had a cropped haircut and a neatly trimmed goatee and was focused on the biker's arm. On the side of his neck was a black tribal tattoo.

"I'm Dan, the owner of the shop," the tattoo artist announced, not even looking up from his work.

"D-dog," the man in the chair chanted in a baritone voice as if urging him on like a cheerleader.

"Nickname," Dan replied, lifting the buzzing tattoo machine away from the biker's arm. He wiped the skin with a rag he held in his other hand. "Are you here for a tattoo?"

"Good god no," Gina replied. "I hate needles."

"It's not a needle, it's a pin," Dan explained, returning the buzzing machine to the biker's arm, who I had to give props to for not even flinching.

"Still a sharp pointy object," Gina insisted. "That's why Sydney and I don't have any tattoos."

I remained silent, causing Gina's eyes to dart towards me.

"OMG, do you have a tattoo?" she asked.

"That's not important right now," I said, shifting my focus to Dan. "We wanted to ask you about a specific tattoo." I turned my phone screen towards him. "We were wondering if you created this design?"

He quickly glanced in my direction, barely noticing the screen at first, then his head snapped back in a double take as if something in the picture caught his interest. The buzzing tattoo machine fell silent.

"Interesting ink," he remarked, abruptly placing his machine on the top of a blue metal tool chest beside him. He slid off his latex gloves and removed the phone from my hand, scrutinizing the image.

"Where did you see this tattoo?" he inquired.

"It belongs to... an acquaintance of ours," Gina said hesitantly.

"How old do you think the tattoo is?" I asked.

Dan pointed at the screen. "The scabbing you see around the edges indicates it's a relatively new tattoo," he explained. "The pink square outline around the outside of the tattoo that resembles sunburn is from the removal of the clear plastic dressing that we apply after a tattoo is complete. It's meant to stay in place for 4-5 days."

He swiped his finger across the screen and moved to the previous picture, then glanced up at me. "This guy is dead," he stated. "Is he the tattoo owner?"

I nodded. "We found the body this afternoon."

"Where did you find him?"

"Floating in the creek at the docks," Gina said.

He nodded. "Makes sense why the scab is white and wet looking."

"We were hoping you could tell us the name of the guy who owned the tattoo," Gina said.

His eyebrow shot up. "Not an acquaintance after all." He paused for a moment. "I was off Sunday, but Mark was here. Kena, come here please."

The young woman, who was dressed in all black, came around the corner.

"Do you recognize this tattoo?" Dan asked, holding the phone up so she could see.

She shook her head. He scrolled back to the previous picture. "How about him?"

She squinted and leaned into the phone. I wondered if she might need glasses.

"Is that guy dead?" she asked. Before anyone answered her, she stated. "I recognize him. Mark tattooed him on Sunday."

"Can you pull up his file on the computer and give these ladies whatever information they need." He handed the phone back to me, pulled on a new pair of gloves, and within seconds, the telltale buzz of the tattoo machine started up again.

"Thank you," I said.

He quickly nodded his head before returning his attention to the man in the chair.

We followed Kena to the desk where she started clicking away on the computer keyboard.

"His name's Casey Stewart. He arrived at one o'clock that day, and he paid in cash. That's all I've got," she replied.

"Thanks for your help," I said.

As we walked back down the street, an unsettling thought kept nagging at me. "Did you find Dan's behavior odd?"

"How so?"

"You didn't mention that you were a private investigator or that we were investigating a case, yet he was willing to divulge any information we wanted."

"So?"

"I have found that no one is that forthcoming unless they are hiding something," I said.

"Maybe Dan is just more laid back than others."

I wasn't sure about that. I had this nagging feeling that this wasn't the last we would see of Dan.

CHAPTER 15

We departed town and headed towards the mountain. Eventually, we drove past the entrance to the marine camp. It had only one road leading in with a gate and a small building with two guards on watch. We drove past the base and stopped half a mile down the road at the spacious parking lot, where a sign greeted us, stating, 'Appalachian Trail.' We parked in a quiet corner and surveyed the area. I noticed markings for several hiking trails heading in different directions that disappeared into the woods beyond.

Once we exited the car, I removed the paintball gun from the trunk. Unfortunately, Gina had left behind her duffel bag of unknown, terrifying goodies, so we didn't have a bag to conceal the gun. After making sure the coast was clear, we grabbed the paintball gun and made our way to the trail that was closest to the base.

No sooner had we stepped onto the path than a young woman met us with a black pug that trotted happily beside her. The small dog barked at us, and Gina, in an attempt to divert the woman's attention, knelt down to pet it.

"It's so cute, what's its name?" she asked, engaging the woman in a conversation.

I ignored the woman and dog and kept walking, holding the gun perpendicular to my side, as I tried to conceal it from view. Gina caught up after several minutes.

"Do you think she spotted the gun?" I asked her.

"No, I distracted her with the dog."

We continued along the well-trodden path for several hundred yards before veering off into the dense woods. I attempted to pull up a map on my phone to guide us, but there was no cell service. I oriented myself, then headed in the direction I knew we should go.

"Are there bears in these woods?" Gina asked as we trudged through the thick underbrush.

"I don't know," I replied, stopping to hold back a low-hanging tree branch for Gina to pass. "You tell me."

"I've never seen one." She suddenly halted, catching me off guard and causing me to bump into the back of her. "I know there are snakes, but what about coyotes?"

"Seriously? You stopped to ask that question?" I stepped around her and resumed my pace.

"Aren't you worried about running into a wild animal?"

"Coyotes, and snakes, and bears. Oh my," I teased.

"You're so funny."

One hundred fifty feet ahead, I spotted the barbed wire atop the fence, which gleamed in the sunlight. We slowed our steps as we approached until we were a hundred yards out, at which point we slowly made our way north, careful not to make any sound that might betray our presence. We continued walking until we spotted the presidential vehicle, which had an armed Marine standing guard beside it.

"They are really taking security seriously," Gina whispered as we crouched down behind a bush.

"With everything that has been going on recently, can you blame them?"

I lay flat on my stomach on the cool, damp ground and propped the gun up to eye level, aligning the sights. "Are you ready?"

On the opposite side of the bush, Gina crouched low where she had a clearer view and removed a pair of binoculars from her purse. "Why can't I do the shooting?"

I pulled back from the sights. "Seriously?"

"You're not the only one in the family who can shoot a gun."

"I know that," I said. "But you are not exactly known for that particular talent. Didn't you shoot your cousin Tom last year with an arrow?"

She huffed. "It was just in the leg. It was hardly fatal. Besides, he shouldn't have been that close to the target."

"I heard he was twenty feet away."

"Whatever," she said with a dismissive wave.

"When I need to blow something up, you will be the first person I call," I replied.

"Got that right," she said, now peering through the binoculars. "I'm ready."

With my arms resting on my elbows and the gun supported by my shoulder, I peered down the scope and zeroed in on my target. I slowed my breathing and aimed at the center of the wheel. I took a deep breath and as I exhaled, I pulled the trigger. The pop that came from the gun discharging was barely audible above the sound of the birds chirping.

"Not bad," Gina said. "You're off 1 MOA to the left."

MOA was a military term meaning minute of angle. It was a way to relay to a shooter how far off the shot was from the target.

I recalibrated my aim accordingly and took another shot. The ball soared through the air, striking the wheel well of the front tire. I was too far away to hear the sound, but the ball splattering against the wheel must have startled the Marine, who glanced around with a look of confusion.

I grimaced. "I'll wait until he moves to the other side of the car to hit it again. We need at least two paintballs to stick to get a good signal."

After several minutes that seemed to drag on forever, the Marine moved on and walked around the car. When he was halfway down the other side of the vehicle, I pulled the trigger in rapid succession and shot out two more paintballs.

He hurried over to our side of the vehicle once again. After inspecting the paint on the vehicle, he scratched his head, unable to pinpoint the source of the sound. The radioactive metal in the paintball blended seamlessly with the chrome wheels. Carefully, we backed away until the fence faded from view.

"Now what do we do without WIFI and a map?"

"So," I said, stepping into the woods.

"We'll get lost."

"Didn't they teach you to navigate in the Army?"

"I was trained in a different skill set," she replied. "My training wasn't about navigation. I just followed soldiers like you to find my way from one place to another."

I shook my head and pointed towards the sky. "The base is west of town. It is almost sunset, so if we head away from the sun, we'll find the path. "

We navigated through the tree without any trouble. As soon as the dense woods opened up, the sun started to dip behind the mountain. As we came around a curve in the trail and approached the parking lot, my heart sank at the sight of Blake leaning against his patrol car. It was parked next to Gina's Mustang, whose yellow paint showed like a beacon in the setting sun. His arms were folded across his chest, and a scowl darkened his features.

"A call came in about two women hunting in the woods," he said as we drew near.

"Dog woman narced on us," Gina whispered in my ear.

"Imagine my surprise when I spotted your car in the parking lot," Blake continued, not looking a bit surprised.

I was thinking we needed a more inconspicuous vehicle. Gina's bright yellow mustang stood out like a lighthouse beam.

"What were you shooting?" he asked.

"Deer."

"Raccoon."

We said in unison.

Blake ignored Gina and fixated on my response. "You're hunting deer out of season?" His brow crunched up in anger.

I turned to Gina. "There's actually a season for hunting deer?"

She shrugged, obviously unsure of the answer.

Blake closed his eyes and pinched the bridge of his nose, a telltale sign of his irritation with me. "Do you have any idea how much trouble you are in? You could go to jail."

"Wow, hunting season must really be a big deal," I replied.

"Hand me the gun," he said, extending his hand towards me.

I handed over the gun and watched as his eyebrows shot up in surprise at its unexpected light weight. He inspected the rifle.

"This is a paintball gun," He exclaimed, his voice laced with surprise.

"Of course it is," I replied.

"Why?"

"I just wanted to practice my target shooting."

"So let me get this straight? You were shooting deer with paintballs?" he said as if he couldn't wrap his head around why anyone would even think of something so ludicrous.

I place my hand on my chest in mock offense. "You don't think I actually wanted to kill one of those poor innocent creatures, do you? I could never kill one of those majestic beings," I said. Human yes. Animal no. Although I was seriously considering snuffing out Cagney and Lacey. Out of the corner of my eye, I caught a glimpse of Gina, her lip caught between her teeth, struggling to stifle a laugh.

Blake stared at me as if he wasn't sure if I appeared in town from Europe or Saturn. He finally handed the rifle back to me.

"Just go," he muttered, shaking his head.

I couldn't help but chuckle at the absurdity of it all. I guess there were no laws against paintballing a deer in the middle of July.

* * * *

We stopped by the hospital to check on Sean. He was sleeping when we arrived. Krista said he was doing much better but he still didn't remember the shooting. We brought her up to speed on what we had uncovered so far.

"I swear you two are like dead body magnets," she said. "What's your next move?"

"Well," Gina remarked, casting a side glance at me. "I thought it would be a good idea to take another look at the victim's car."

I shot her the evil eye. "And I reminded her that it was in a police lock-up."

"That hasn't stopped you before." Krista reminded me.

"I thought you were the rational one in our little trio?" I asked.

"Usually," she replied, her gaze drifting to the doorway of the hospital room. "But this time it's my husband."

I felt the guilt of promising Krista I would find Sean's shooter. So far, I hadn't been able to deliver. "Fine, but you definitely can't come," I said, looking directly at Krista.

"Oh, I plan on coming this time," She replied.

I sighed. "No, if you're caught with us, it won't just be Sean who faces the consequences. They'll think you both are involved, and those two state troopers will scrutinize every detail of his life as if it were under a microscope."

Her shoulders slumped. "You're right," she admitted. "Just... be careful."

"Always," Gina replied.

Who was she kidding? We were anything but careful.

CHAPTER 16

The police impound was located just outside of town. We arrived shortly before midnight. As we drove past the lot, my eyes were drawn to a small white shack beside the main gate, its windows dark. There was a single pole light in the center of the lot, which cast a warm glow across the gravel that tapered off into the shadows at the edges.

The metal gate firmly shut, secured with a heavy chain and padlock. A stark white sign was affixed to the gate stating "Police impound No trespassing" in bright red letters. If there hadn't been a camera mounted at the corner of the guard shack pointed at the gate, I would have picked the lock and slipped in that way.

The houses along the road were scattered over several acres. Two properties down from the impound, stood a large two-story house with two separate driveways. One ran directly in front of the house, and another led to an oversized garage at the far corner of the lot, which was hidden from view. We decided to park there.

We crept around to the back corner of the lot, where we were hidden in the shadows. Gina had pulled a pair of large wire cutters from her back seat before we left the car, and I used them to snip away at the chain-link fence with precision. I formed a C-shaped hole, then carefully maneuvered the jagged wire out of our path.

"Watch out for the sharp edges of the cut wire," I warned as I squeezed my way through the opening in the fence.

Gina followed closely behind, but suddenly paused, her voice laced with panic. "I'm stuck."

I rolled my eyes. "I don't know why I even bother to warn you," I said as I went back to unsnag her from the fence.

"Not all of us are as thin as you," she shot back, holding still so I could examine where she was caught.

"I prefer the term slender."

She glanced down at her arm, her expression changing to concern. "I cut myself." A deep scratch marred her skin, glistening with blood that was now seeping from the wound.

"I'm shocked," I replied as I grabbed her shirt above the area where it was stuck. I yanked hard on the fabric, which tore away with a loud rip. Gina wiggled away from the fence and then turned to inspect the damage to her shirt, the remnants of fabric hanging loosely around the gash.

She sighed. "This was my favorite brown shirt."

"That color shouldn't be anyone's favorite," I replied. "I did you a favor."

The lot was spacious enough to accommodate nearly three dozen vehicles, but currently only held about two dozen, accompanied by a bright blue Kawasaki Ninja motorcycle.

"Nice bike," I remarked, taking a moment to appreciate its sleek design and glossy finish. I noticed the car from the hardware store's parking lot was parked next to a truck.

"I'll check the trunk if you want to look around the interior," Gina suggested.

I checked both side doors, and there were no exterior locks. "There's no lock for me to pick."

"No problem," Gina replied confidently. With a swift motion, she swung the wire cutters she still held in her left hand and smashed them into the driver's side window with a resounding crack. Glass, shattered and fractured into a spiderweb pattern before falling like glistening raindrops. "There, the cars open."

"Stealthy," I replied, reaching in and unlocking the door with ease. Leaning down, I pulled the trunk latch for her.

Starting with the glove compartment, I rummaged through it, finding only the car's rental agreement inside. Not surprising, the name on the document was John Smith. "Rental car," I said to Gina.

"Figures."

There was nothing in the center console, and I was just about to slide my hand under the seat when I heard an "Oh no," from the back.

I crawled out of the car and made my way towards the open trunk. "Did you find something?" I asked as I rounded the back.

The ETD machine was turned off and silent, resting in the middle of the trunk, but Gina had her penlight fixed on the back corner.

"I don't see anything," I said.

"Look closer," she urged.

I leaned deeper into the trunk and spotted nothing but the gray carpet that lined the interior. "There's nothing there."

"That's because you don't know what you are looking at." Gina pushed me aside. She then stuck the tip of her finger in her mouth and touched the spot in the truck where her light was honed in. When she withdrew her finger, she illuminated its tip. "Do you see the small flakes of white powder?"

"Barely,"

"It's Triantone Triperoxide or TATP. The number one explosive chemical terrorist use in homemade bombs."

"I take it this is bad?"

"This substance is just as strong as TNT."

"And the ETD identified it?" I asked.

Gina shook her head. "Not necessary. The fruity smell was a giveaway. It's highly unstable but effective. Even a small amount can cause serious damage."

I leaned closer, my curiosity piqued. "What is it made from?"

"A mixture of different chemicals," she said, peering deeper into the trunk. "The most well-known ingredient in the concoction is acetone."

"Layman's terms," I said.

Gina sighed. "You're a professional you should know this."

"Your department not mine. Remember I was taught navigation and sharp shooting. You were taught bombs."

"Paint thinner," she replied.

My thoughts raced as I processed the information. "Which is readily available at a hardware store."

"Do you suspect the Faulkner brothers might be involved?" Gina asked.

I nodded. "We did see them at the grocery store when I spotted the Tasqhir tattoo."

Just then, a car halted in front of the gate, nearly blinding us with its piercing headlights. We instinctively ducked down behind the car. The harsh sound of a metal chain scraping against the fence poles echoed in the stillness. I exchanged a quick, tense glance with Gina. Without hesitation, we darted two cars down and hid out of sight.

"Did you see someone when we pulled in?" a male voice asked.

I groaned when I recognized the voice belonging to Trooper Grant.

"I think you're seeing things," Rhode replied.

"Really? Then why is the trunk of the Nissan open?"

I heard their footsteps pound against the gravel as they rushed towards the car. The hole we'd made in the fence was too far away for a quick escape without drawing attention. My mind raced, weighing our limited options, none of which looked good.

I pulled my phone from my pocket and handed it to Gina. "Head toward the hole in the fence," I whispered. "If I don't make it out, bring the screen to life and push and hold the number three."

Before she could respond, I began to stealthily slip around the far corner of the compound, maneuvering between the parked vehicles, careful to remain hidden from sight. The sudden click of flashlights pierced the air. I saw their beams cutting through the darkness, sweeping across the lot.

I froze in place as I was almost caught in the light, as I attempted to dodge from one car to another. As I crouched down, I felt a sharp sting as a small rock embedded itself into my palm sending an electric shock up my arm. I snatched up the rock and hurled it towards a vehicle that sat four cars away, which connected with a ping.

"Did you hear that?" Rhode asked as I heard their footsteps drawing near. Peering cautiously around the truck's bumper, I could see them. Gina seized the opportunity to sneak towards the exit. Unfortunately, she wasn't as quiet as a mouse, and I heard a metal clang coming from her direction.

Both troopers swung their flashlights around.

I exhaled in frustration, knowing I had to do something. I bolted from my hiding spot behind the wrecked truck into the open, racing towards another vehicle, knowing there was no way they would miss seeing me.

They caught my movement from the corner of their eyes. Their flashlights swung in my direction, but they were not quick enough to catch me in the beam of light. I dove behind a white box trunk and then quickly rolled underneath it. I lay motionless, my breathing slow and controlled as I heard the gravel crunch just inches from my ear. They paused for a moment before continuing their search, their footsteps fading away.

I couldn't help but roll my eyes at their lack of awareness. My gamble had paid off as they moved away from Gina's location. My relief was short-lived as I realized they were now moving closer to the hole we had created in the fence.

"What do we have here?" Grant inquired as his flashlight started scanning the fence.

I cursed under my breath as I heard a faint rustle to my left. Gina edged her way towards the main gate, likely hoping the trooper's attention would remain fixed on the hole they were investigating at the back of the fence.

Unfortunately, her foot snagged on an unseen object, sending her sprawling face-first onto the ground, eliciting a sharp gasp and a woosh from her. She now lay in the open.

I knew what I had to do and rolled out from under the truck. Before the troopers spotted Gina, I stood up with my arms raised above my head. "You got me," I declared, which was the biggest overstatement of the year. If we were trapped in this impound lot for a week, I had no doubt I could easily evade capture from these two officers.

They rushed towards me, their flashlights trained directly on my face, and I diverted my gaze to escape the blinding glare.

"I'm not surprised to see you," Trooper Grant sneered as Rhode began to frisk me.

Grant's eyebrows shot up as Rhode removed my gun and pocketknife. Rhodes maneuvered my arms behind my back and handcuffed me. As they proceeded to read me my Miranda rights, I scanned the lot and Gina was nowhere in sight. They loaded me into the back of their patrol car, then we headed out of the lot towards the police station.

Chapter 17

A short while later, they led me into the interrogation room of the police station. I didn't spot Blake as I was ushered through the building, and a wave of relief washed over me. Hopefully, he was at home, asleep, and unaware of my presence here.

I was unceremoniously deposited into a stiff, wooden chair before they informed me that they would return, shortly before closing the door behind them. The room was small, suffocating, and devoid of windows. The sparse furniture consisted of a stainless-steel table and two additional chairs, positioned across from me. Dominating the wall in front of me was the stereotypical large one-way mirror. The room had no smell, but the air felt stagnant. The space was meant to feel claustrophobic and evoke a feeling of fear. It was meant to feel like a trap and toy with the minds of those who found themselves here.

With my line of work, this was not the first time I had been arrested, and the anxiety I was supposed to feel wasn't going to happen. I pushed against the chair, and it didn't budge. I figured it was bolted to the floor. From experience, I understood that this was the waiting period where prisoners were supposed to worry and fret over their fate. With no idea of how long they intended for me to remain here, I decided to entertain myself.

I rolled my neck feeling the tension depart, then did the same with my shoulders, loosening them up. Rising to my feet, I moved my arms down to the back of my thighs, then sat back down. With deliberate effort, I lifted my legs, sliding my arms down the back of them and repositioning them in front of me.

Glancing at my reflection in the mirror, I waited in the brightly lit room. After several minutes of no one entering the room, I suspected that there was no one on the other side of the glass watching my every move.

I shook my head, the corners of my mouth curling upwards. "Amateurs," I muttered under my breath as I propped my feet up onto the table.

I reached into my left boot and felt the cool metal of my lock pick. When I touched the uniquely shaped handle of the right one, I pulled it out of my boot. My lock picks were specially designed for me, and this particular one's handle was shaped like a handcuff key. Holding it firmly, I expertly maneuvered it into my restraints, and within seconds, I was free of the handcuffs. With my hands free, I placed the pick back in its hiding place, then crossed my ankles casually on the table and leaned back in my chair as if I were relaxing in the comfort of my own home.

Closing my eyes, I allowed myself to drift into a light slumber, figuring I could get a little sleep while I waited. In the military, you learned to sleep whenever you got a chance. I had no idea how long I had been asleep when I was disturbed by the sudden creak of the door. Troopers Grant and Rhode stepped into the room, effectively shattering the quiet.

They pulled out the chairs with deliberate slowness. Settling into their seats, they fixed their gaze upon me, their expressions inscrutable as they remained silent. Ah, the cold, silent treatment. A tactic intended to make me squirm and sweat. I fought hard not to smile. I had once withstood twelve grueling hours in a Turkish interrogation room with no food or water, not even a bathroom break, and spoke not one word. I had faith they would crack before I would.

To pass the time, I directed my attention to the ceiling and started counting the tiny holes in the white ceiling tiles. I made it to five hundred and twelve when Grant finally broke the silence.

"What were you doing in the impound?" he asked.

Rhode leaned forward. "What were you hoping to find in that car?"

I said nothing. My gaze drifted to the mirror, as I wondered if someone was silently observing from the other side.

After several moments of silence, Grant continued. "What is your brother-in-law's involvement?"

My eyes shot to his, and a surge of determination coursed through me. I slowly uncrossed my ankles and withdrew my legs from the table. Leaning forward, I placed my uncuffed hands on the polished surface and intertwined my fingers.

Both troopers exchanged glances of surprise at my unrestrained hands, but they chose not to comment on it.

"Sean has nothing to do with what's going on," I stated.

Grant leaned forward, his voice casual but laced with authority. "What is going on and how are you involved?"

I leaned back and pulled my hands from the table, continuing my silence.

"We can sit here as long as it takes until you tell us what you know."

Suddenly, the door to the room swung open with a loud bang, slamming against the wall behind it. A man in his early thirties with neatly styled sandy blonde hair, wearing a navy t-shirt and jeans, strode into the room. A smile broke out across my face at the sight of him.

"You can't just walk in here. We're in the middle of an interrogation," Grant said to the intruder.

"Not anymore," the man replied, his tone smooth and confident.

"You can't be her lawyer?" Rhode spat with barely concealed disdain. "She hasn't even been given a phone call yet."

"Oh, I'm much worse," the man said, casting a glance my way and giving me a nod. "Sydney is leaving with me."

Grant shot up from his chair, the sound of its legs scraping sharply against the polished floor echoed through the room. "No, she is not. Ms. Hayes is under arrest. She's being charged with trespassing, burglary, and destruction of police property. With further charges pending."

The new guy in the room was Curtis Byers, my partner. His eyebrows arched, and he shot me a questioning glance. I simply shrugged. We had been working together in the counterintelligence unit for so long that he had learned to accept the unpredictability of my antics without batting an eye.

"Sydney is an officer in the Army," Curtis said. "Therefore, she is the property of the United States government. You have no jurisdiction over her."

I couldn't hide the smile on my face as I stood. I casually tossed the handcuffs on the table in front of Rhode.

"You can't just take her," Rhode barked. "She's hindering our investigation."

Curtis ignored him and reached into his wallet, removing a business card. "Send the bill for repairs to this man," he instructed, handing the card to Rhode. "He'll reimburse the cost of repairs. He's Sydney's commanding officer, so if you have any complaints, you can address them with him." Curtis gave me a knowing smile before he returned his attention to the now dumbfounded troopers.

"I assume you confiscated Sydney's gun," he continued with authority. "She'll need that back."

"No way," Grant said, his tone dripped with smug satisfaction as he crossed his arms defiantly over his chest. "She may be military, but she doesn't have a permit to carry a concealed weapon in Pennsylvania," he glared at me. "We were planning on charging her for that, too."

Curtis cast a sidelong glance in my direction which I met with an innocent expression. He cocked his head to the side and gave me a stern look.

"Fine," I conceded and flopped back down in the chair. I rested my right foot on the edge of the seat and untied my laces. I slipped off my boot and reached into a hidden pocket, withdrawing a yellow plastic card. I handed it to Rhode.

He scanned it before his eyes widened in disbelief. "This is a federal weapons carry permit," he said. "I thought only military police and federal agents carried these." His gaze narrowed as he scrutinized me. "How is it that a simple nurse has possession of one?"

"That is no concern of yours," Curtis replied. "Please return her weapon to her."

Rhodes left the room while Grant stood with a dark expression, looking like he wanted to shoot us both. I had just finished lacing up my boot when Rhodes returned with my firearm in one hand and a vanilla envelope in the other. I tucked my gun securely in my waistband before plucking the envelope from his hand. With confidence, I followed Curtis out of the room.

We didn't speak until we slid into the leather seats of his car.

"Nice BMW," I remarked. "How can you afford this on a government salary?"

"Cut the crap," he shot back, turning the key and bringing the engine to life. "Andrews is going to have both our heads when he finds out about this."

Colonel Stanley Andrews was my commanding officer. He was a stickler for the rules and would undoubtedly erupt when he learned that I had almost been arrested.

"Thanks for coming," I said.

"I was a little surprised when I received your emergency call in the middle of the night, especially when I heard Gina's voice on the other end. You're just lucky they haven't deployed me back to home base yet." During the drug raid where I had been shot, Curtis had broken his arm in two places. Though he no longer wore a cast, I suspected that he was still on military leave until he was fully healed. In our line of work, not operating at one hundred percent could mean the difference between life and death.

"I do have to say it was fun seeing the look on those cops faces when I informed them you were coming with me." His face broke into a smile. "Now, tell me what on earth made you break into a police impound?"

During the rest of our drive, I filled him in on everything we had uncovered and shared my suspicion about what lay ahead. His brow furrowed, the creases growing deeper with every detail I revealed.

The front porch light was on as we pulled into the driveway. Gina was pacing restlessly on the porch. As we exited the vehicle, she jumped off the porch and ran over, playfully punching Curtis on the shoulder with mock annoyance.

"Curby, what took you so long?"

Curby was Curtis's military code name. Everyone in the special forces had one. His was chosen as a mix of his first and last name, Curtis Byers.

Curtis gave Gina a one-armed hug. "Nice to see you too."

"I can't believe the crap you get yourself involved in even when you're off duty," Curtis said, shaking his head. "Why don't we hit the hay for now? I'll call Andrews in the morning and debrief him. We can hash this all out then."

I led Curtis to the spare bedroom before retreating to my own room. Feeling the weight of exhaustion settle over me, I flopped down onto the bed. I fell into a deep sleep before I even had time to kick off my boots.

The feeling that I hadn't slept at all encompassed me as I sprang up in bed, adrenaline coursing through me as I gripped my pistol tightly and aimed it toward the door. I listened intently but heard nothing. My senses were always on high alert, honed by years of vigilance, so I knew without a doubt that an unexpected noise had jolted me awake.

The room was still pitch-black, indicating it was the middle of the night. Then I heard it, a faint rustling sound drifting up from downstairs. I crawled out of bed as I stealthily made my way towards the stairs, alert to any further disturbances.

As I descended into the dark depths, a faint light flickered from the kitchen, most likely from the fixture over the stove or pantry. I plastered myself against the wall and slowly stuck my head around the doorframe. I had been right, it was indeed the pantry light, and I could hear someone rummaging inside.

With my gun aimed steadily at the pantry opening, I cautiously rounded the corner. Gina emerged carrying a hammer in one hand and a crowbar in the other. She was dressed from head to toe in black and sported a determined look on her face.

I knew Gina well enough to recognize what she had in mind.

"Give me a minute to run upstairs and grab my phone," I said before dashing out of the kitchen.

CHAPTER 18

We parked on a side street a block away from the church. The street was calm and quiet, with no soul in sight. Father Michaels believed that anyone should be able to confess their sins to the Lord whenever the urge struck them, so he kept the front door unlocked at all times, which made breaking into the church too easy.

As we opened the door, it swung silently on its hinges, allowing us to sneak into the chapel. "How exactly do you plan on silencing the bell?" I whispered as we crept down the shadowy side aisle next to the pews. I personally had no idea how a bell operated beyond the simple mechanism that made it chime as the thing in the middle of the bell hit the side.

"It must run on some kind of clock system since it rings exactly at the hours."

"And you know how to break a clock?" I shot back.

"I broke my wristwatch once when I dropped it into a swimming pool," she replied.

"Did you bring a bucket of water with you?" I teased.

"No, but I did bring a vial of nitroglycerin with me."

If that statement had come from anyone else I would have thought they were joking, but I knew Gina was serious.

"You can't blow up the bell," I stated firmly.

"Last resort," she replied.

We stood at the back of the chapel, its flickering candles casting shadows against the walls. To our left was a wide area featuring three doors, each leading to a different area.

"The door on the left is Father Michaels office," Gina said.

We opened the door in the center, revealing a narrow hallway with stairs at the end that dropped off to the basement.

"I never realized the church had a basement," I said.

"The sleeping quarters are most likely down there," Gina replied.

We closed the door and moved on to the furthest door from the other two. Behind this door we discovered a steep staircase leading upwards.

"Bingo," Gina said just before a sudden sound caught my attention.

I whipped around and saw Sister Mary Sarah standing by the open door we'd just closed.

"Gina, Sydney?" she asked puzzled, her gaze dropping to the hammer in Gina's hand and the crowbar I was now holding tightly.

"Thank heavens," she breathed before performing the sign of the cross. "Carry on." With that, she disappeared into the hallway, the door clicking shut behind her.

"Guess we're not the only ones who hate the bell," Gina said.

We climbed the stairs until we reached the top. The massive bell was suspended from a long horizontal pole that was connected to an array of gears and chains. The gears slowly turned as if counting down to the next moment the bell tolled again.

"You work on removing the chains," Gina instructed. "I'll see if I can take out the gears."

I handed her the crowbar and went to work. There was some banging and cursing involved as we wrestled with the stubborn machinery. After what felt like an eternity, we succeeded in halting the gears, and the tower fell silent.

Gina had managed to pry loose two of the gears, which were now scattered fragments lying on the floor. We gathered them and the chain I had removed and exited the structure. On our way home, we pulled into the back parking lot of a closed fast-food restaurant. We dumped our treasures into the grimy dumpster.

"I'll finally get to sleep in tomorrow morning," Gina said with satisfaction as we drove off into what was left of the night.

* * * *

The next morning, I woke up and rolled over, surprised to see the red digital display glowing a bright eight. I was shocked because this was the longest I had been able to remain in bed since arriving in town. Sitting up to stretch, my stomach immediately started to grumble. Breakfast, I decided, would be my first order of business.

As I wandered downstairs, I noticed no one else was up yet. Opening the refrigerator, I cringed at the sight of a lone loaf of bread and a pack of bacon. We really needed to do a better job of stocking food. I pulled the bread and bacon out, contemplating the morning meal. Usually, Gina cooked eggs in the morning to accompany the bacon.

I surveyed the backyard and spotted Cagney scratching enthusiastically at the grass and pecking at the ground. Her tiny feet flung bits of dirt behind her. I didn't see Lacey, so there was a good chance she was still nestled in the coop.

I shook my head and turned away from the window. There was no way I was taking the chance of being accosted by the two miniature feathered dinosaurs before having my morning coffee.

I poured the dark coffee grounds and water into the top of the pot, then pressed the button with anticipation. Being such an expert at cooking, I pulled out my phone and searched for a simple bacon recipe. I settled on one that called for frying the strips in a pan for fifteen minutes. Sounded simple enough.

I pulled out a skillet and placed it on the stove. I arranged a layer of thick bacon in the pan and turned the knob to medium heat as the recipe instructed.

Standing there for a moment, I watched intently, but nothing seemed to be happening. Maybe this was the reason I didn't cook. I didn't have the patience for it. I glanced at the clock on the wall and was dismayed to see that only two minutes had passed.

Being in the military, I had mastered the art of showering and dressing in under ten minutes, so I ran upstairs to get ready for the day.

As I emerged from my shower, the enticing aroma of smoky bacon wafted through the air. A smile crept across my face as I got dressed and laced up my boots. Cooking wasn't so hard after all. I decided to make toast to go with the freshly cooked bacon, and we would skip eggs altogether.

Just as I picked up my gun from the bed, a high-pitched alarm came from downstairs. I dropped the weapon and sprinted down the staircase. Upon bursting into the kitchen, I was met by a disturbing sight. A thin layer of smoke rolled across the ceiling, rising from the stove where the pan was now completely engulfed in flames.

Frantically, I ran to the sink and filled up a glass with water. Just as I was about to throw the water onto the inferno, I felt the glass being magically lifted out of my hand. I turned to find Blake standing behind me. His mouth was moving as he talked, but the wailing of the fire alarm drowned out his words.

I pointed to my ear, conveying my inability to hear him. He frowned as he quickly scanned the countertop. He snatched a towel and used it to grab the handle of the pan. He made his way to the door, unlocked it, and with a swift motion, he hurled the entire flaming contents into the yard outside. The startled chickens took one look at the fiery pan, then waddled off towards their coop as if saying, "Not today."

Blake left the door ajar to vent out the smoke, then returned to the stove and pressed a button on the microwave, silencing the alarm.

"They put smoke detectors on microwaves?" I asked, a bit surprised.

"Yes, for people like you," he replied. "Don't you know it's dangerous to throw water on a grease fire?'

I stared at him blankly.

"Do you even know how to cook?"

"Of course I do," I lied. "That bacon must have been defective. I still had three more minutes until it was done cooking."

"Uh-huh," He responded, leaning against the counter. "And did you leave the kitchen?"

I paused for a moment, debating on telling the truth, but I figured he wasn't going to believe that I sat there and watched the pan catch on fire. "Only for a minute."

He threw his hands in the air in exacerbation. "You're lucky you didn't burn the house down. You never walk out of the kitchen when you are cooking something on the stove."

"Yes, Mother," I replied sarcastically as I inserted two slices of bread into the toaster. Toast would have to suffice for breakfast.

He glared at me sardonically, making me want to slug him in the face. "With Gina and you both living here, you need three smoke detectors in every room and a sprinkler system."

"How did you even get here?"

"The front door was unlocked, which is rather unsafe," he replied.

I sighed. Gina had a habit of forgetting to lock the doors, and I was too exhausted last night to check.

"That's not what I meant," I said.

His eyebrow hitched up.

I placed my hands on my hips. "That may be what I said, but what I actually wanted to know is, why are you here in the first place?"

He crossed his arms over his chest. "I heard that Trooper Grant arrested you last night."

"And," I replied, removing the warm toast from the toaster and inserting two more slices into it.

"Rhode and Grant aren't saying much, but I assume it has something to do with butting into police business. I'm really surprised you're not still in jail."

I glared at him.

"I got to tell you," Blake continued. "I was looking forward to being the first person to arrest you for being nosey and bending the law."

"Do you go out of your way to irritate me?" I shot back.

"Maybe," he said, effortlessly pushing away from the counter.

"Why?"

He took a step towards me. "Because you're cute when you're angry."

In an instant, my anger dissipated, and I had no sarcastic remark waiting on my tongue. Despite the urge to take a step back, I stood my ground as he reached out his hand. My breath caught in my throat as he gently picked a curl from my cheek and swept it behind my ear.

"Good morning," floated a voice from beyond the doorway.

I heard footsteps on the stairs and quickly stepped back as Curtis entered the room. He paused for a heartbeat before approaching Blake.

"I'm Curtis," he introduced himself, extending his hand. "A friend of Sydney's from work. I came into town for the Fourth of July celebrations."

Blake hesitated for a moment then shook his hand.

"Blake," he replied simply, his tone casual as he strolled out of the room making his way towards the front door.

"I hope I wasn't interrupting anything," Curtis said as I heard the front door close.

I stared at the now vacant doorway. "No," I replied. "Nothing at all."

Just then, Gina entered the kitchen with her nose wrinkled and sniffing the air. "Did you burn the bacon?"

I nodded as I glanced out the open door just in time to see Cagney and Lacey now feasting on the charred remnants of our breakfast.

"Done that once or twice," Gina replied as she retrieved the jelly from the refrigerator.

We had just finished our elaborate breakfast when my cellphone rang.

Dominic's voice echoed through the speakerphone. "Good morning, darling."

Curtis looked at me in surprise. "How many men do you have chasing you in this town?" he whispered.

I shot him a scowl.

Dominic hadn't heard him and continued. "The guy with the tattoo, Casey Stewart, was twenty-seven years old and, if you can believe it, still lived at home with his parents." He rattled off the address. "He drove a white Honda Civic and worked at Adams County Realty."

I thumped my palm against my forehead. "Of course, the Casey that's in charge of the short-term rentals." I don't know how we could have missed it. The pieces were starting to fall into place.

"That's right," Dominic said. "I've got to go. I'm at the casino and I'm winning big time." He disconnected.

"So, the dead guy with the Tasqhir tattoo happened to be in charge of rental properties," Curtis said, shaking his head. "There is no doubt the group is holed up in one of those locations. We need to contact Andrews."

I sighed. I knew Curtis was right, but I wasn't looking forward to the butt chewing that would be forthcoming. The Colonel answered the phone on the first ring. Curtis quickly filled him in on the unfolding situation.

After what felt like an eternity of silence, I was sure the Colonel had a massive heart attack and passed out.

"Jesus, Hayes," his voice finally boomed over the phone. "You can't even go on leave in a barely existent town without attracting trouble. How many people have you shot since you've been there?"

I paused while I thought about it, which elicited cursing on the other end of the line.

"I should have locked you in the basement of the Pentagon," Andrews said.

Rolling my eyes, I shot back. "That won't fix the problem at hand."

"No, it won't," I heard him exhale. "Curby, head over to the real estate office. Show them your ID and demand a list of properties and any information they have about who's currently renting them."

"Bopsie twins," Andrews barked. "You two need to steer clear of that office. Last thing we need is for the town to know about your real jobs."

"I'm already retired," Gina reminded him.

"Do you want me to start yelling at you?" Andrews replied. "If the town of Gettysburg knew you were an explosives expert, they'd never sleep again."

He had a point.

"I'll reach out to General Marshall and brief him on the potential situation," he said firmly before ending the call.

"That went better than I thought it would," Gina said.

We both looked at her. It was easy for her to say since she was already retired. However, I was not going to get off so lucky. After this was all over, I was certain Andrews would summon me down to Washington for a reprimand at the very least. Hopefully, they won't boot me out of the military for conducting an unofficial investigation. God help me if he learned about the incident at the funeral home last month.

CHAPTER 19

We dropped Curtis off in the alley one block away from the building that housed both the real estate and Gina's PI business. The plan was for Gina and me to park in the lot behind the building and go to her office while Curtis entered the building via the front door. We would wait in her office in case Curtis needed assistance. As we strolled down the corridor, Curtis entered through the front door.

We were going to ignore him and pretend we didn't know him as planned, but the sign on the real estate office door made us all stop. A black ribbon was painted at the top of a stark white sign. Beneath it was written: "Closed in observation of Casey Stewart's death. Will reopen tomorrow."

"The VP's speech is tonight," I said. "We don't have until tomorrow."

Gina morphed into spy mode. "I'll cover the rear entrance," she said, pivoting towards the back door.

"Curtis," I said, gesturing towards the front entrance.

His brow furrowed as he hesitated. "You do realize you are not on foreign soil and aren't under the protection of the US Army right now?"

We both stared at him.

He sighed. "Fine. Nice to see that you haven't started following the rules or the law while you've been on leave," he muttered under his breath as he turned his attention towards the front of the building.

The door was equipped with a dead bolt, but within a few minutes, I felt a rush of satisfaction as the internal mechanisms of the lock gave way. I slowly eased the door open and peered inside, my senses heightened as I surveyed the surroundings. The office was quiet, and there were no surveillance cameras or alarm systems to betray our presence. Without hesitation, I quickly entered with Gina hot on my heels.

"I'll keep a lookout," Curtis said before I gently shut the door behind us.

Gina handed me a pair of black latex gloves. I didn't have to worry about my prints being on the doorknob since we were here just the day before. I headed towards what I assumed was Casey's empty office from our previous visit. I pressed the Enter key on the keyboard perched on top of the desk, and a password prompt popped up on the computer screen. Meanwhile, Gina began rummaging through the drawers.

I removed my phone from my pocket and dialed Dominic. He answered on the fourth ring, his voice thick with sleepiness.

"Are you still sleeping?" I asked.

"Some of us are on vacation," he replied.

"I need to break into a computer that's password-protected."

"Whose?" he asked with curiosity.

"Casey's. I don't have time to explain it right now."

"Fine," he responded with a yawn. "Are there any picture frames on the desk?"

I scanned the nearly empty desk. "No."

"How about a paper weight?"

"There's nothing on his desk but the computer," I said. Irritation crept into my voice as I felt the pressure of time and didn't understand the relevance of the questions.

"Flip the keyboard over," Dominic instructed patiently.

I internally rolled my eyes but complied. My annoyance turned to surprise as I spotted a small handwritten note taped to the bottom of the keyboard. I typed the words from the note into the keyboard, and the screen flickered to life.

How did you know?" I asked.

"You'd be surprised how often people write their passwords in obvious places," he replied. "They're the same kind of people who think a fake rock in the flowerbed hiding a key is fooling anyone."

As he guided me through navigating the maze of files, I felt a wave of relief wash over me when I finally landed on the document containing the list of short-term rentals. I thanked him for his invaluable help.

"No problem. I'm heading back to bed now," Dominic said as he hung up.

I pressed the print button on the computer, then realized the room lacked a printer. Glancing around, I noticed the printer was sitting on the table in the conference room.

"I'll get it," Gina said as she made her way towards the exit. However, she misjudged the entryway and collided face-first with the transparent barrier. Instinctively, she raised her hands to brace herself. The entire wall seemed to jiggle and sway like Jell-O. For a moment, I feared the whole structure was going to collapse.

Gina pulled back from the glass, a surprised expression on her face, as she grabbed her nose. I exhaled the breath I was holding when the wall stopped moving and stabilized. Gina pressed the side of her nose tentatively and winced.

"I hope I didn't break my nose," she said.

"I'm just glad it's not bleeding," I replied. "The last thing we need is for you to leave a blood trail behind."

"Thanks for the sympathy," she said sarcastically.

"If you were paying attention to where you were going, it wouldn't have happened," I said, striding past her towards the conference room. "See if you can find some paper towels and glass cleaner."

"Really?"

"Yes," I replied, pointing to the now imprinted face and handprints that adorned the glass." Your face is now smeared on the wall and you left behind your fingerprints. It looks like a crime scene."

With an exaggerated huff, she headed to the back of the office to search for supplies. I quickly scanned the printout, then folded it before stowing it in the side pocket of my cargo pants.

After Gina cleaned the glass, she tossed the used paper towel and window cleaner into her purse. "Happy?" she said as we exited the office together.

* * * *

"We need to compare these rentals to a map so we can narrow down the choices," Curtis said from the backseat of the Mustang as he placed his mirrored sunglasses on his face.

Fortunately, there were only about forty properties on the list, but even that felt like an overwhelming number to sift through in one day.

"An actual map of the area would be easier than trying to look at one on the laptop," he added.

Gina shot me a knowing look, and I nodded in agreement as we cruised out of town toward the farm. The landscape shifted from bustling streets to sprawling fields. When we arrived, I spotted Pap's legs peeking out from under the front of his Durango. The moment he heard the car doors slam shut, he wheeled himself out from beneath the vehicle.

"What are you doing?" Gina asked.

"Just finished with an oil change," Pap replied, wiping the grease from his hands with a well-used rag.

"We need a map of the entire town that extends past the airport," Gina said.

Pap nodded, understanding the urgency of our request, and we headed into the barn. We moved towards the box of maps he had left sitting on the floor beside the workbench. Curtis removed his sunglasses and placed them in his shirt pocket.

Pap popped the top of the first cylinder he retrieved, and we helped him unroll it across the table. The map was so large that it completely occupied the entire workbench. As we hastily grabbed tools to weigh down the corners, my father entered the barn.

"I saw you pull in," he said as he approached the workbench. "Figured you were up to something. Luckily for you your mother is out getting her hair done." His gaze drifted down to the map that was sprawled across the tabletop. "What are we looking for?"

As I retrieved the crumpled list of rental properties from my pocket and unfolded it, we quickly filled Pap and Dad in on the details of the case.

"So, you now have a dead guy with a tattoo from a known terrorist organization inked on his arm, and you're thinking the terrorists are holed up at one of these locations," Pap summarized.

"Pretty much," I replied.

"Who's the bloke?" Dad asked, nodding his head toward Curtis.

"Curtis Byers," Curtis replied, leaning across the table to shake Dad's hand.

Pap rubbed his chin thoughtfully. "Name sounds familiar." Then he snapped his fingers. "I got it, Curby, you're Sydney's partner."

It was nice to know that even in retirement, Pap was still keeping tabs on me.

Curtis nodded.

"Have you been keeping my Sydney in line?" Pap asked.

"Ha, the entire army can't keep her in line," Curtis replied.

"Can we get back to the matter at hand?" I said. "The clock is ticking."

Pap snatched the list from my grasp. "We can eliminate any apartments or townhouses. They wouldn't want to be too close to their neighbors."

"Agreed," I said as Curtis and Gina nodded.

"There's probably a bomb involved," Gina said. "I discovered bomb making residue in the trunk of the car where we found the first body."

"So, we need to pinpoint a location where a bomb could be detonated, as well as a concealed site for any potential unfriendly fire or a sniper as backup," I suggested.

"Exactly," Gina said.

At that moment, the sharp ring of Curtis's phone sliced through the air. "It's Andrews," he announced before putting it on speaker.

"Yes sir," I said.

"It's a no-go," Andrews replied. "General Marshall called the Secret Service, and they shot it down. The director of the Secret Service made it clear, and I quote, "I'm not altering our plans based on the rantings of an Army sergeant on vacation."

"Really?" Gina replied.

"Without proof, we have nothing," Andrews growled. "Do you have proof?"

"Working on it," I replied.

"Work harder," he barked before abruptly disconnecting the line.

"You heard him," Pap said, his tone steely as he took charge. "Here's the Marine base where the VP's vehicle is currently being housed, and here is the airport he will be flying into." Pap pointed out both locations on the map.

Pap's finger drew a line along a road towards town. "This is the most logical route they will take to get to town. If there's a bomb, it's going to be set somewhere along this path."

We were all huddled around the worn map, following the route with our eyes as we strategized the most effective location for an ambush.

"I think the bomb will be set in town, ready to detonate as soon as he steps out of his car." Gina proposed.

I scanned the printed road, my eyes darting back and forth, searching for the ideal spot. Suddenly, clarity struck me. "No," I said. "There." I pointed at the Rock Creek bridge.

The group exchanged skeptical glances.

"It's the only bridge on the route into town," Gina pointed out. "They'll check it thoroughly shortly before they leave."

"Yes, but what if the bomb isn't actually on the bridge itself?"

Curtis's brow furrowed. "I'm not following."

"If they are in a rental house along the river, they could load the bomb onto a small boat and time it perfectly to pass under the bridge the moment the SUV crosses over it."

Pap tapped the map with the tip of his pen. "Not a bad idea. They could station someone near the airport to keep an eye out and notify them when the VP's caravan pulls away."

"There are always plenty of fishing boats on the creek," Dad said. "One more wouldn't raise any red flags."

Curtis nodded. "I'm sure one of the terrorists would be willing to carry out a suicide bombing. His name would go down in history."

"There's just one problem," Gina interjected as she pointed at Pap's Durango. "The new presidential vehicles aren't just bulletproof, they're bombproof. Nothing short of a nuclear weapon will breach that armor."

I leaned forward, placing my hands on the map.

"They don't need to blow up the vehicle itself," I argued. "If they take out the bridge, the water is deep enough to submerge the SUV. Once it hits the water, they'll have to evacuate."

"Which makes them easy targets for gunmen," Curtis added, a serious tone resonating in his voice.

Gina's eyebrow shot up in surprise. "They'll be sitting ducks."

"Brilliant," Dad exclaimed. "Now we just need to focus our house search to the ones along the creek."

Pap glanced over the property list. "The east side of the creek is part of the forestry preserve, so there aren't any houses there." His pen danced across the page, circling several addresses. "There are five properties on Front Street."

Dad leaned in, peering over his shoulder. "The odd-number houses are on the water side, so you can eliminate 416 from the list."

I chimed in, tapping my finger on the map. "The house will be upstream of the bridge. That'll make for an easier launch and trip."

Pap scratched another house off the list. "That leaves us with three options."

I paused, mulling it over. "I don't think it will be this house," I said, pointing at the southernmost house.

"Why not?" Gina asked.

"We assumed Casey was killed at the boat dock, but what if that's not where he died?" I said. "What if he was murdered at the rental house first, and then his body was discarded in the creek to cover up the crime?"

"And instead of sinking to the depth of the creek bed, he washed up at the boat launch," Gina said, frowning. "Don't terrorists know how to weigh down a body to prevent it from floating?"

"They didn't have to," Curtis replied. "Even if the body was found, who would suspect them?"

"No one but us," I said.

Pap glanced at the crumbled paper in his hand. "We're left with 483 and 571."

"Then that's where we're headed." I said. "We'll split into two groups."

At that moment, the sound of gravel crunching under tires reached my ears. I looked out to see Krista's car pulling in. She hopped out and ran towards the barn, ran as well as she could run in two-inch heels.

"How can I help with the investigation?" she asked.

Curtis shot her a skeptical look. "Does everyone in town know about this case?" he asked.

I gave him a don't be stupid look. "This is my sister, Krista," I said before turning my attention to Krista. "We were just getting ready to leave."

"Not without me," she insisted with a look of determination.

I paused for a moment, weighing my options. As long as I could find a role for Krista that kept her out of harm's way, I didn't see any reason to exclude her.

"Okay, you and Dad head over to the airport," I directed. "Time how long it takes to get from the airport to Rock Creek bridge. Let Dad drive since he drives faster than a snail, so that we can get a more accurate time."

Krista stuck her tongue out at me, then followed Dad to her SUV.

"Gina and Pap," I said, turning toward them. "You two take the boat and scan the backyards from the water. See if there's a boat docked at either place. Just try to be inconspicuous."

Pap nodded.

"We'll check out the houses from the street," Curtis said.

I glanced over the vehicles parked nearby. "We're going to need a car," I said.

Pap rummaged through his pocket, finally producing a set of keys. He tossed them to me. "Take the Durango. With those tinted windows, they'll never spot you."

Pap grabbed a couple of well-worn hats off pegs on the wall, then picked up two fishing rods.
We stepped outside, each of us heading off for our assignment with purpose and determination.

CHAPTER 20

Curtis eased down Front Street, the wheels slowly rolling across the asphalt. Each house on the block mirrored the next in its two-story design, yet each had its own unique siding and shutters.

"Looks like Smurf village," I remarked.

"Huh?"

"You know every house is the same mushroom design just splashed with a different color." We stopped in front of the first house, which was void of life or any sign of movement. No vehicle graced the driveway.

"Maybe they're in town for the festivities," Curtis suggested.

"Let's not cross this house off the list just yet," I replied.

We continued our drive two blocks further down the road to the next house. As we approached, I spotted a man slumped down in a chair on the front porch, his cowboy hat pulled low over his face like a shield. He gave the illusion of sleeping, except I noticed his head turning slightly, hinting that he was watching us as we passed.

At the back corner of the house, I caught sight of a lone figure hiding in the shadows. He appeared to be of Middle Eastern descent, and he leaned against the building, remaining almost indistinguishable from the darkened backdrop. His gaze followed us intently until we vanished from view.

Bingo, we had a winner.

I relayed a description of the two men to Curtis.

"I didn't get a clear look into the backyard," I said.

"Let's head back to the barn and wait for the others," Curtis replied as he turned sharply at the next corner.

We were the first to return to the house. By the time Gina and Pap arrived, there were only a few hours left before the earliest possible arrival time of the VP.

"It's 571 Front Street," Gina announced as soon as she stepped into the barn. They were the last to arrive back at the barn.

Pap nodded and huffed softly as he struggled to keep pace with her.

"There were two men loading duffel bags into the bottom of a bass boat and another man standing guard at the corner of the house," he said, a little short of breath.

I nodded in agreement. "That's probably the man I spotted. There was another one pretending to sleep on the front porch."

"That accounts for at least four enemies that we know of," Curtis said.

"They all paused and turned to stare at us as we floated past," Gina said. "But we kept our fishing lines in the water and played it cool, pretending not to notice them."

I nodded.

"Isn't there some sort of thermal imaging device like in the movies," Krista asked. "One that can help us see how many people are inside the house?"

We all looked at her, and Pap responded, "Only government-grade tech."

"We would need an aircraft," I said.

"And we'd need to fly within fifty yards of the house," Curtis added.

Krista threw her hands up in exasperation. "Geez, I was just asking. A simple 'no' would have sufficed."

"I'm calling Andrews," Curits decided, reaching for his phone.

"Good work," Andrews said after Curtis elaborated on our findings. "This should provide enough evidence to push for the cancellation of the Vice President's trip and bring in the Feds."

"What do you want us to do in the meantime?" I asked.

"Hold tight," Andrews instructed. "This is a Secret Service problem."

"I thought international terrorism was part of our job?" Curtis asked.

"Yes, internationally, but you're on home soil now. Besides, the two of you are on leave, so get back to resting so you can return to work." Andrews hung up abruptly before we could respond.

"Not big on long conversations is he," Gina remarked.

"I don't know what the rest of you think, but I'm staying right here until this thing is neutralized," Pap declared.

Everyone nodded in silent agreement. Pap unlocked a heavy wooden door in the barn. Pap and Dad stepped inside, and after a few moments, they emerged, each carrying a handgun, and Dad held a rifle equipped with a scope.

"Just in case," Pap announced as he placed his gun on the table. He began loading bullets into the magazine with practiced efficiency. From his pocket, he produced two extra nine-millimeter clips along with a handful of bullets and handed them to me. "In case you need extra."

Curtis arched an eyebrow and peeked around the doorframe into the shadowy room beyond. "Your Pap and Dad have a weapons room? Your family's so cool," he exclaimed.

It was after seven when my cellphone buzzed. I frowned as I glanced at the name flashing on my screen, and without hesitation, I put the call on speaker mode.

"I can't get through to General Marshall," Andrews voice crackled through the phone. "I tried General Page, but he cursed me for interrupting his night and hung up on me."

"That doesn't surprise me," Pap replied with a knowing smirk. "He's probably out with his mistress."

"I called Camp David, and Lieutenant Moore is sending a troop, but they're over an hour out," Andrews added.

Curtis glanced at his watch. "I don't think we have an hour. The speech is scheduled for eight thirty."

Andrews let out a long breath. "Do what you have to, and I'll cover for you. But if you're wrong, I'm denying all knowledge of your actions."

"Thanks for your vote of confidence," I replied.

"Hayes," Andrews added. "Stay safe and for once be careful."

I looked at Pap, "You're the highest-ranking officer here. What are your orders?"

Pap shook his head. "I'm retired. I think Curtis and you should take charge."

"Alright Hurricane," Curtis said, addressing me by my callsign. "You're in charge."

I quickly assessed our options, my mind racing with what was at stake.

"Gina, hand the tracker to Dad," I instructed, then turned towards him. "Do you know where the hiking trails are down Woods Road?" I wanted Krista and Dad to be as far from any potential danger as possible.

Dad nodded. "Past the reserve camp."

"There's a tracker on the presidential vehicle," I said. "As soon as you see the dot on the screen move, text me."

Gina turned on the device and handed it to him, its small screen glowing in the evening light.

"You put a radioactive tracker on the presidential vehicle," Curtis said, shaking his head in disbelief. "Oh, yeah, we're going to jail."

I ignored him. "The rest of us will head to the house."

Pap, Curtis, and I piled into the Durango, anxiously waiting for Gina as she retrieved a bag from her car. She tossed it into the back seat before sliding in beside me.

"Do I want to know what's in there?" I eyed the bag with apprehension.

"Just some emergency supplies," she replied, but I noticed Curtis inching closer to the door. He was well aware of Gina's infatuation and its potential complications.

As we drove past the house, we noted that the sentry was no longer stationed on the front porch, and the individual at the corner of the house was gone.

Curtis flashed me a knowing look. We both understood what this meant. Either the team was geared up to move, or worse, had already taken action. The urgency in my gut told me our window of opportunity was closing fast. Pap pulled the Durango to a stop at the corner of the block.

"You two stay here," I instructed Pap and Gina as I opened the door to exit.

"We want to help," Gina protested.

I shook my head firmly. "You aren't trained for this type of work. The best thing you can do is call the police if you hear any gunfire."

Gina and Pap exchanged worried glances but said nothing further.

Curtis and I snuck around the side of the neighboring house, praying that no one was home. As we crept along the side, I withdrew my gun from my waistband. Cautiously, I peeked around the corner and spotted two men near the boat at the creek. One man was armed with an assault rifle, while the other was hoisting something over the side of the boat. This one was carrying a device that resembled a detonator. I scanned the surrounding area but didn't see anyone else. Time was running out, and there wasn't room for hesitation. We would have to wing it.

I nodded to Curtis before sprinting across the neighboring backyard towards a tree with a trunk wide enough to shield me. As soon as I stepped into the open, the man with the rifle locked eyes on me. Before he could raise his weapon, a gunshot rang out from behind me. The rifleman crumbled to the ground, lifeless. The other man, realizing the danger, quickly yanked his leg back from the boat and dove down for cover.

"Don't move," I shouted as I peered around the trunk of the tree. I caught sight of two hands popping up into the air, followed by the figure of the man standing beside the boat. I scanned the backyard, but no one emerged from the building.

I nodded to Curtis, who promptly sprinted across the yard and ducked behind a shed at the back of the property. He trained his weapon on the man by the boat. I rushed over to one of the duffel bags still on the ground and unzipped it. Sure enough, it was filled with packed plastic bundles of white powder explosives.

Just as I was about to circle the boat to apprehend the terrorist, a squeak echoed from the back door.

Without hesitation, I dove headfirst behind the shed as a stream of bullets ripped through the earth mere inches from where I had been standing.

"Nice move," Curtis remarked, as he took post at the shed's corner. I crouched on the opposite side, adrenaline coursing through my veins.

The sound of footsteps thundered down the stairs of the house, accompanied by a stream of shouting in Arabic.

The man by the boat began to drag it into the water.

I was torn. Shooting at the boat to sink it would mean risking an explosion that could take us all out in the blast. I leveled my gun at the guy tugging on the boat, but the moment he caught sight of me, he ducked down behind the vessel.

He shouted to the others in the yard, and suddenly, a spray of bullets erupted, tearing through the shed, causing us to duck down. I fired a blind shot around the corner of the shed, hoping to discourage our attackers from advancing any closer.

"Reminds me of Bagdad," Curtis said with a smile.

"Obviously, you and I have a vastly different recollection of that experience," I replied. Reaching over, I snagged his mirrored sunglasses from his pocket. I positioned them just right to scan around the corner of the shed. Through the reflective lens, I caught sight of two men armed with AK-47s. One of them looked familiar, but I couldn't quite place him.

"Give up. There's nowhere to run," he said, and then it hit me. It was Philip, the other real estate agent, whom we met for the first time when we stepped into Adams County Realty. Gina had handed him her business card, which meant he knew she was a private investigator. It dawned on me that knowing a PI was looking for Casey, made him a liability, which is why he was eliminated. Philip most likely is the one who not only killed Casey but shot Sean.

Another flurry of bullets shredded the shed, punctuating the knowledge that we had limited time. There was nothing else in the yard to hide behind, and unless there was some heavy metal object inside the structure, there was nothing to prevent them from turning the shed and us into Swiss cheese.

Before I had time to formulate a plan, the high-pitched whine of a small engine pierced the air. Through the lens of the sunglasses, I spotted a sleek black and emerald green RC car zipping across the yard. Taped to its top was a cylinder grenade.

I dropped the glasses and turned to Curtis. "Flash," I warned as I squeezed my eyes shut and cupped my hands over my ears.

Even though I was hiding behind the shed and facing away, a brilliant light flared behind my closed lids, seconds before the deafening explosion erupted. As soon as I heard the bang, I rounded the corner of the shed and shot Philip in the shoulder right before unloading another round into his kneecap. I heard Curtis firing his gun at the same time, and both assailants crumpled to the ground. I dashed forward and kicked Philip's gun away and leveled my weapon at him. Curtis sprinted over to the man he had shot and checked him for signs of life. Once he confirmed he was still alive, he expertly secured both of their hands behind their backs with zip ties.

Philip glared at me with hate in his eyes.

I kicked him in the gut, eliciting a moan. "That's for Sean."

"Why don't you just kill me," Philip replied.

"I'd rather see you charged as a traitor to your country," I replied.

Gina rounded the corner, clutching the RC controller in her hand. The tension in the air was palpable.

"You'll never be able to stop us," Philip spat.

I ignored him and locked my gaze on Gina, a surge of frustration coursed through me. "Why didn't you stay in the car?" I asked. Images of what could have happened to her if the situation had gone differently flashed through my mind. "I gave you a direct order." I glanced over my shoulder, and the boat was already in the water, drifting downstream. I cursed under my breath.

"I had to do something to help," Gina replied.

"No, you didn't," I shot back. "You could have been killed. Why would you take that chance?"

"Don't you know?" she said. Her expression softened as she tilted her head. "You're my ride or die."

Despite my anger, a smile tugged at my lips. Gina and I had always shared a closeness, but in that moment, I realized just how much our bond had deepened over the past few months since I returned to town.

My phone vibrated in my pocket, and I had no doubt about who it was. It could only be a message from Dad.

"The target is on the move," I said. "Gina, can you guard these two? Shoot them if they even sneeze."

"Got it," Gina responded as she pulled a gun from her purse. The barrel was so long it would have made Dirty Harry proud. "Go ahead, cough."

Curtis and I wasted no time and took off towards the Durango that was now idling at the curb in front of the house. We both hopped into the backseat as I yelled, "The boat's on the move."

Pap slammed down on the accelerator, and the vehicle leapt forward before the door was even closed.

"How are we going to stop the boat now?" Curtis asked as we sped out of the neighborhood and down the winding road. The thick trees on the side of the road cut off the view of the river.

As we approached a curve, the tires shrieked in protest. We leaned into the turn, and I feared we might topple over. In that instant, it was clear that Gina's reckless driving habits clearly ran in the family.

"Maybe we can reach the bridge first and block it off," I suggested.

"There's a clearing up ahead," Pap replied, his voice steady despite the urgency of the situation.

Abruptly, the dense tree line gave way, and I spotted the Presidential caravan of three black SUVs cresting the hill half a mile away. "We'll never make it to the bridge before them," I said, dread creeping into my voice. I saw the boat careening towards the bridge. "Over there," I exclaimed. "There's the boat. But it's too far away to get a clear shot."

Without warning, Pap slammed on the brakes, causing me to tumble off the seat and slam into the back of his seat.

"Lift the trunk pad," Pap ordered. "Hurry." He pushed a button, and the sound of the moon roof opening filled the vehicle.

I felt around behind the seat, my fingers grasping two black pull tabs. I folded back the carpet, and my eyes widened in disbelief.

"This vehicle comes with a missile launcher," I exclaimed, as I carefully extracted it from the trunk.

"God, I love your family," Curtis said.

I stood on the back seat, adrenaline surging through me as I poked my head out of the roof. My gaze darted to the river where the boat drifted down the middle of the stream. Curtis handed me the rocket launcher as the Presidential caravan started across the bridge. I knew I had only one shot.

I aimed at the boat. The man on the board caught sight of me. I could see the shock wash over his face, his eyes widening in disbelief as I pulled the trigger. A sharp hiss erupted as the rocket shot forward, hurtling toward its target like a hungry cheetah. It struck the boat with a deafening blast, shattering it into a million pieces about fifty yards from the bridge.

The vehicles on the bridge skidded to a halt and slowly started backing up. I noticed two men sprinting towards the vehicles on the bridge, rifles gripped tightly in their hands. I knew the armored SUVs would protect the occupants.

I let out a sigh of relief just before a bullet ricocheted off the roof inches from me. I dropped into the safety of the backseat. Several men whose tans weren't from the sun started to advance toward our vehicle.

A moment later, a low rumble was coming up the road from behind us. I peered out the window just as a dessert tan six-wheeled military cargo truck thundered past us. To my surprise, I caught a glimpse of Church sitting in the passenger seat. He waved as they surged forward.

Ahead of us, the vehicle came to a halt, and a half dozen armed Marines in full combat fatigues poured out of the back and hurried off after the terrorist who started to flee. I could hear the crack of gunfire in the distance.

Curtis opened the door. "Get out of here. I'll take care of this."

"Are you sure?" I asked.

He nodded as he pulled his weapon from its holster before dashing off after the Marines.

"Don't fret," Pap said as he shifted the vehicle into gear. He turned it around, steering us away from the escalating confrontation. "I think you sufficiently saved the world for one night."

* * * *

We all met back at Gina's house, where we could decompress and enjoy some coffee while we shared the details of the evening's events. Gina, however, couldn't shake off her disappointment. She spent a good five minutes pouting and sulking over missing the final event of the evening.

"I can't believe you blew up a boat without me," Gina grumbled. "And with a rocket launcher of all things."

"I promise next time I have an urge to fire a rocket," I said, chuckling at her dramatic flair, "You'll be there." Of course, I had no plans to ever fire a rocket again, but she didn't need to know that.

"This was great," Krista said, her eyes sparkling with excitement. "I can't wait to tell Sean all about it."

The three others at the table exchanged knowing glances before looking at Krista.

"What?" she asked. "Why are you all looking at me like that?"

Having served in the military at various points in our lives, we understood the gravity of our covert operation. It was a reality that the details of an event like this could never reach the ears of the general public.

"You can't tell Sean or anyone else about what transpired tonight," I said.

"You're kidding, right?" Krista retorted. "I was part of a team that saved the Vice President's life."

Gina shook her head. "It's like Vegas. What happens on a mission stays on the mission."

A silence fell over us at the weight of her words and the unyielding code we were obligated to uphold.

"The government is going to view this as a Secret Service screw up and they'll do everything in their power to keep it under wraps." Pap finally declared, crossing his arms over his chest. "And no member of my family is going to cause a leak regarding this story."

"But the news is going to know there was an explosion on the creek," Krista replied.

"They'll cover it up," Curtis said. "Most likely blame it on a gas leak on a boat."

"Besides," Gina added. "With Sydney's job, her name can't be mentioned in connection to this at all."

Krista exhaled in frustration. "So that's it. We just pretend it never happened and don't discuss it again after tonight?"

"Pretty much," I replied.

"That blows," Krista said. "The most exciting thing that ever happened to me and no one will ever know."

I gave her a knowing smile. "Welcome to my life."

CHAPTER 21

The next day was the Fourth of July. Curtis arrived early in the morning to retrieve his car as he needed to head back to DC for debriefing. After he left, Gina and I spent the day relaxing on her front porch, enjoying some lemonade as we relished in the quiet now that the church bell had ceased its ringing.

That evening, as the sun dipped in the sky, Gina and I made our way to the park for the celebration and fireworks. At the edge of the park was a large, open field where everyone gathered to enjoy the fireworks launched from the adjacent baseball field. The parking lot was filled with food trucks of all colors, lined up along the curb. With the windows down, the aroma of the food wafted in, with scents ranging from smoky barbecue to fragrant curry.

Just as Gina parked the car, my cellphone rang, pulling me from the festive atmosphere. I frowned when I saw a blocked number on my screen.

"Go ahead, "I told Gina. "I'll catch up." She closed the door with a slam and sprinted towards the array of food trucks.

Not knowing who was calling, I hesitantly lifted the phone to my ear.

"Sydney Hayes?" a deep voice inquired on the other end.

"Speaking," I responded.

"This is Vice President Al Harman."

"Yes, sir," I said, and even though he couldn't see me, I instinctively sat up straighter in my seat.

"I'm not going to beat around the bush," he continued. "I understand I have you to thank for saving not only my life but the lives of my Secret Service agents."

"Yes, sir," I repeated. I hadn't prepared for a call like this, and the notion that the VP took the time to reach out left me stunned.

"I wanted to thank you personally," he said. "I heard you're on medical leave, yet you still put yourself in danger to save me. I'm in your debt. If you ever need anything, give me a call."

"Thank you, sir," I replied, knowing this would be my last conversation with him.

"You are an invaluable asset to our government, and I'm certain the military can't wait for you to rejoin your team. Goodbye," he concluded, the line fading to silence.

I pulled the phone away from my ear and stared at it a moment in contemplation, struggling to grasp my unpredictable emotions. When he mentioned my return to service, I didn't feel the usual exhilaration I always felt in the past. For the first time, I felt a heavy sadness. There was a sense of dread in the realization that I would have to leave not only Gina and Krista but also the town itself. During my time here, I reconnected with old friends and forged new bonds. Would I truly be able to walk away from my family and Gettysburg as easily as when I was a headstrong youth?

Not only that, I felt I had done some good while I was here. Maybe not enough to change the universe, but enough to make a difference in this little corner of the world. My thoughts were abruptly interrupted by a prickling sensation at the nape of my neck, and I knew someone was watching me. I turned my gaze toward the side window and saw Church leaning casually against a sleek black Harley. I hopped out of the car.

"I was surprised to see you last night," I said, strolling over to him. "I thought you were out of the military?"

"Semper Fidelis," he replied with a glimmer of pride in his eyes. This was latin for 'always faithful.' The Marines embodied the idea an interpreted as, 'once a Marine, always a Marine.'

I paused a moment, then looked him in the eye. "How did you know?"

A lopsided grin crept across his face. "My buddy D-Dog recognized the tattoo you showed him. Called me the moment you left his shop."

Curiosity rose inside me and I couldn't suppress the question. "Was he with you last night?"

'D-dog was driving." His half smile expanded into a full grin. "We figured you could use a little help."

So, D-dog was a Marine. He was most likely stationed in the Middle East during his Marine tour if he was able to recognize the significance of the tattoo inked on Casey's arm. Gina spotted us from across the parking lot and made her way towards us.

"Until next time," Church said before turning on his heels and heading towards the crowd mere seconds before Gina arrived.

I turned to Gina. "What do you know about him?" I asked, still watching Church's retreating figure. "He never says much, but he carries a presence that's hard to ignore."

"I know that he can get me anything I want and never asks questions," she replied.

That was comforting.

She grabbed me by the elbow. "Come on," she urged, pulling me along behind her. "I'm starved."

We decided on a truck adorned with the Mexican flag painted on the side. After we ordered tacos, we meandered over to the beverage truck and treated ourselves with iced caramel lattes.

Gina had already laid out a blanket in the grassy field, so we settled down to enjoy our meals. As we ate, I took a moment to observe the crowd. The lawn was filled with colorful blankets and an assortment of lawn chairs. As the sun began to descend behind the mountain, the children's laughter filled the air as they darted around with sparklers.

"I should get us some sparklers," Gina suggested.

I shook my head. "It's a holiday. No fires or ER visits tonight."

There was a low murmur among the crowd as the twilight of evening faded away into night.

"I want some funnel cake," Gina declared, standing up.

"Grab me one," I called out as she walked toward the truck.

At that moment, the fireworks show kicked off with a single firework that hissed as it soared upward, erupting into a brilliant white flash that illuminated the night sky, followed by a thunderous bang that silenced the crowd.

After that, a cascade of colors began to fill the darkness from vibrant ruby reds to deep sapphire blues. Each ending with shimmering gold flakes that fell back to earth, while the breeze swept aside the puff of smoke.

I felt the blanket shift beside me as I turned in anticipation of receiving my funnel cake. I was taken aback to find Blake sitting next to me instead of Gina.

"Enjoying the show?" he asked as he leaned back on his hands and crossed his ankles.

"I was," I replied with a sardonic smile.

"Are you trying to goat me, Army?"

I shrugged. "How are the state troopers making out with Sean's investigation?"

"They're not," he replied. "First thing this morning, two federal agents walked into the station and took over the case. They made it clear that the troopers assistance was no longer needed, then they walked back out of the station. The troopers headed back to their own barracks."

"I guess that gave you a sense of satisfaction, considering the way the troopers treated you."

"I did enjoy that part," he admitted. "But now that the feds are in charge of the case, we'll never uncover the truth of what really happened."

I nodded, concealing the knowledge I held about the events that had transpired.

"I don't see your friend," Blake said, referring to Curtis.

"Something came up," I replied. "Curtis had to return to DC."

Blake leaned forward, his gaze lifting towards the night sky where a brilliant orange firework erupted.

"I like you, Sydney," he confessed, turning his gaze back to me, sending my heart racing. "But I won't ask you out."

At that moment, a small piece of me felt the pang of disappointment while the rest remained bewildered. I furrowed my brow. "Okay," I replied, questioning where this unexpected conversation was headed.

"You're not a nurse are you?" he asked.

"What makes you say that?" I replied, trying to maintain a casual demeanor.

He nodded towards my attire, his eyes flicking over my combat boots and the pocketknife clipped to the outside of my shorts. "You carry a pocketknife everywhere you go, and you have martial arts training from your youth that I doubt is going to waste. Whenever you sit in the diner, you position yourself with your back against the wall and survey the crowd with vigilant eyes, as if looking for threats. Not to mention you run towards danger instead of shying away like any sane person would."

I remained silent as his gaze returned to the fireworks overhead. He continued. "Besides, there was a big event at the corner of town last night with gunfire in two locations and an explosion. When I arrived, the Secret Service had closed it down and wouldn't even let us near it. Now your friend, who had just arrived in town, has mysteriously vanished after last night's incident."

"I believe trust is an essential part of any relationship," he continued. He stood up and looked down at me. "I can't ask you out to dinner if I don't know who you really are." With a slight nod, he turned and walked away, leaving me alone.

As the vibrant colors of the fireworks bloomed in the sky, I found myself lost in thought, wondering if I even knew who I was anymore.

Gina approached me, beaming as she handed over a warm funnel cake on a delicate paper plate. The golden brown pastry was generously dusted with powdered sugar, making my stomach grumble in anticipation.

As the sky lit up in a kaleidoscope of colors during the grand finale, Gina turned to me and asked, "Have you enjoyed your Fourth of July?"

I pondered for a moment, my gaze fixed on the dazzling display overhead. "It's hard to say," I replied. "What I do know is this night has given me a lot to think about."

Follow Misty Lynn at – mistylynnbooks.com

Facebook: Misty Lynn-Books